Thank you ...
for your suppo...
By C.T.

LIKE

LUST

LOVE

Relatable short stories about relationships and emotions

By C. Taylor

Edited by Dominique Lambright

LIKE. LUST. LOVE

Printed in the United States of America

First Printing, 2019

ISBN 9781980389620

Battle Creek, Michigan

C.T.

This is a work of fiction. Names, characters, places and incidents either are the product of the author's imagination or are used fictitiously, and any resemblance to actual persons, living or dead, business establishments, events or locales is entirely coincidental.

Intro

Hello, I am the one and only Ms. Dasia Lovelace. I am a 28-year-old African-American woman from Detroit, MI. I stand 5ft 8 inches tall, with brown eyes, a peanut butter skin complexion, thick thighs, an excellent personality, freaky enough, and successful. Plus, I have that A1, wet wet, good good, they say. However, we will discuss this later.

For some time now, I have struggled with finding the right man for me. In the words of Katt Williams, I said to myself, "You need to figure out what's wrong with you and your pussy." I have had good and bad experiences with men. There were those I liked, those I lusted over, and those I loved. Of course, there were those who reciprocated my feelings and those who may have just

3

fucked me and said, "Fuck your feelings Dasia." Maybe not directly intentionally but sometimes it felt that way.

Now, let me take you on my journey to reach Endless Love Blvd. Honestly, I had to ride down Sucker For Love Street and a few other roads to get on the right path to my goal. To find that true, never-ending love story is the goal. Like. Lust. Love will have you comparing your life to some of my most intimate short stories/relationships. It starts with puppy love and ends with that, "I want to spend the rest of my life with you love". If you have an affinity for sex, love, drama, and reading...You'll love this book.

Chapter 1 - My First Lust

His name was Shawn Feltner and he played football for Ferris St. University. He was 19 and I was only 16. The year was 2003. This man was sexy, with a chiseled physique like a grown man. Compared to some of the other girls my age, I still felt like my shape wasn't poppin' yet but he was still attracted.

When I first met him, the smell of his cologne heightened my attraction. Whew, I remember that scent oh too well. Shawn was 6ft 3 inches, and 200 lbs. of muscle with a chest that screamed lay on top of me, eyes that said, I promise you won't regret it, and lips that whispered, "Let me get that pussy." Shit. I damn near want to Google his ass right now!!!

Now let's be honest here, a good majority of people lost their virginity right around this age. I hate when people front like, "She was a hoe at sixteen", "Where was her home training?" ...Don't even go there people. Curiosity killed this cat very quickly...lol...I digress.

I met Shawn in my freshman year of high school while I was at a track competition. It was a two-day meet, so the whole team stayed the night in some hotel rooms instead of traveling back home. Once the second day of events were complete, we all went out to eat. While returning to the hotel, there were a couple of cuties in the hallway. It was me, Michele, Jas, and Tisha in my room, so we were bound to have something crazy happen because we were a mess together.

So, to make a long story short the guys asked if they could come by later and we said yes, knowing damn well that if a coach caught us we would probably get kicked off the team. It didn't matter because we were daredevils. When they came by everybody introduced themselves and basically each female picked a guy. There was four of us and three of them. They got there around 9pm, but I couldn't tell you what happened the rest of the night because I was so into talking to Shawn. I found myself almost staring at times!

I do remember him walking around with a camcorder asking everybody their names and I said I was DL, he said, "So you sneaky on the down low huh?" and we both laughed.

"Nope, it's my initials." And from there it was like magic. He asked how old I was, and I said 17 getting ready to turn 18 (lies). He said he was 19 and we just clicked.

The level of comfort was scary, but we exchanged numbers before he left and quickly started a long distance relationship from there.

Even though Shawn was the star on the football team, he was a down to earth guy. He called me every morning and night, and came to visit several times before the big day. It never failed that almost every time we were out on a date, there would be females jockin' him so tough. Some ladies flirted right in front of my face! There were those that even had the audacity to ask questions like, "Why are you with that little girl?" and his reply would be, "This is my woman." I loved that dumbfounded look on their faces, because it was priceless every single time.

Truthfully, it was my own personal secret that was boosting my confidence. As of today, I never told Shawn I was three years younger than him. When we met I told him I was 17 and was getting ready to graduate from high school. Don't judge me. You all have done this before.

One night I had met him at a hotel suite right after one of his big games. I lied and told my mom that I was staying that night at one of my homegirl's cribs. I planned to tell him my secret that night, but unfortunately I could never find the right moment. When I approached the door he had already instructed me to get the key from under the doormat. I followed his orders and cautiously entered the room where he had candles lit, the lights dimmed, and he was fully nude in the hot tub. I began to walk in and he says, "Stop." So I did, and he then said, "Take off all of your clothes."

Now I had never had a man speak to me like that before, so for a few seconds, I

9

was speechless. After gathering my thoughts, I said, "Come take them off for me." With no towel, he steps out of the hot tub, walks toward me with his body dripping water, and let's just say it was ON. Facing me he drops to his knees and slowly removes my shoes, pants, and panties. Sensually and seductively he planted small kisses from my ankles to my thighs. I found myself doing something I had never done before, moaning. All I could think about was that if this is sex, I want to do it every chance I get, hahaha. He lowered me to my knees and removed my shirt and bra. Using both hands he squeezed my C cup titties together and sucked the left nipple then the right nipple then left again, and right. By this time, I felt as though my heart was beating to the rhythm of an R&B tune.

My womanly fluids were formulating. This turned me on. I wanted him to feel it, so

I said, "Touch it." He put his thumb across my clit and I quivered. I was scared and anxious all at once. I was a virgin! Right on the floor he laid me on my back, spread my legs apart and tongue kissed the pussy. In a harmonizing fashion, he grunted, and I moaned in ecstasy. Five minutes after oral sex he begins to slowly enter me. It was a coincidence that Intro's "Come Inside" was playing from the boom box.

"Damn I can't get it in and you are super wet, don't tell me this is your first time?" he said. I nodded my head yes. He pulled back, sat up, and asked, "Are you sure you want me to be your first?"

I lifted up towards him, and in the sincerest voice I could find, I said, "YES!" I braced myself and slowly guided him inside of my lake of love, I meant lust. After just a few strokes he stops and puts on a condom.

Unfortunately, the sex only lasted about eight minutes and he was done. As he laid curled up on the bed snoring, I laid flat on my back taking in every detail of what had occurred. Honestly, I was surprised that I went through with it, but I was more interested in me liking everything but the actual act of penetration. However, it was only my first time so I knew no better.

Shawn and I continued dating for several more months. We never had sex again but that didn't stop him from trying every time we were together. I eventually matured and realized that I was wasting my time. More so, I was ready for something or someone different. As time went by I often daydreamed about our sexual encounter. To a certain extent, the thought of having sex with him aroused me. However, my thoughts were only about the sex and not necessarily any

long-lasting feelings for Shawn. I was
wondering if he could pick me up like the
men in the pornos, or if he could make me
scream like the women in the movies. To be
direct and explicit, I was wondering if it
would be more pleasure than pain if we did it
again, and possibly if I could stand to get on
top. Even as a teenager I was smart enough to
know that I may have fallen in love with the
idea of intercourse but not in love with my
ex-boyfriend, which was ok because I had all
my life to fall head over heels in LOVE.

Chapter 2 - I'm Feeling Myself

By my early 20s, things were going great for me in my life, especially regarding a career, men, and relationships. I was blossoming into a beautiful woman and I had just finished my Bachelor's at Wayne State University. Directly after college, I received a great position at HOT 107.1. You couldn't tell me nothing. I was young, black, sexy, educated, employed, freaky, sporty, single, and more. I'm feeling myself a little too much right now huh?

Anyways, around this time I was rolling with my bitches, my girlfriends, the homies, my besties. Normally you wouldn't catch me out without one of my BFFs. Even though I had a lot of confidence in myself, that all seemed to disappear if they were around or least I pretended as if it did. They helped to develop me into the woman I am today. They are always there with relationship advice. Always encouraging me to pursue my goals (even when they aren't pursuing their own). They even give a few freaky tips here and there too. Most importantly, they are my confidants, despite the fact that sometimes we don't talk as much; but we are always there for each other whenever one may need an ear. Let me describe them to you really quick.

First you have Michele, who's super thick, works part-time at a bank, and is a huge flirt even though she is married. She loves attention and believes she holds all the top secrets and treatments for keeping a man. Next is Foxy, who's about 5ft 5in tall, peanut butter complexion, pretty eyes with a ghetto/supermodel/spoiled woman attitude. On the flip side she has a college degree and works at the city council building downtown off Jefferson, so she is making her own bread, even though she never spends it. She always seems to find the tricks or ballers… No matter what, I love them like sisters. Our bond is over 10 years strong.

Swear I used to do childish stuff like have one of them walk over to a man in the club and tell him I was interested. If he approached me then cool, and if he didn't I just had them move onto the next guy. Even though I claimed to be so confident, I still bullshitted like that! I could never sweat a guy, but I was and have always been one who knows what she wants, without getting others approval. That's what's wrong with women nowadays, always waiting on a friend to dictate their next move. It may sound contradicting, but hopefully someone catches my drift. Your homegirls may damn near talk you out of your relationship, or have you missing out on a great guy because he doesn't meet their standards. Like I said before, "find out what you want". I digress.

At first, St. Andrews was our spot, then we got older, our money got longer, and our taste in men changed so you found us at Lucky's or another joint over on Telegraph. We used to enter the club with not a dollar in our pockets and drink all night. Trust and believe that we could buy the bar all night, which we did multiple times but there used to be so many dudes all in our faces willing to cash out. Personally, I ignored half of them. I was just a flirt. It used to excite me or be something of a challenge to see if I could get the hottest guy in the club to notice me. He didn't have to ask for my number, or to buy me a drink or to dance. He only had to give me enough attention to let me know that I

17

could have him if I wanted him. That was okay with me, but my homegirls would often be like, "Girllll you better talk to him." Sometimes I would follow their suggestions and other times I would do my own thing.

Chapter 3 - He Likes Me

Just for the record T.I. is one of my favorite rappers in the world. One of my favorite lines of his is that, "One thing about your feelings is this, you can't change em'," but often we follow our hearts and ride with our emotions, which can lead you straight down Sucker for Love Street. Trust and believe, I have gone down this road once or twice. On this street you will find temptation, materialistic things, false ideologies, and generic love.

I met a guy not too far away from Sucker For Love Street. I should have known not to fall for anyone from that area. He was about 5ft 11in, 180 lbs., average build, light skin, pretty eyes, and decent hair. When he approached me he simply stated, "I'm in a rush, if possible can I please have your name and number and maybe we can get to know each other over lunch or something?"

His appearance was okay, so I gave him my number and watched him as he walked away and got in on the passenger side of his homeboy's ride. What a joke. Michele whispered, "Scrub," in my ear, but I laughed it off and kept it moving. Any thoughts of pursuing him should have been canceled, but his approach seemed genuine and original and I couldn't seem to resist.

By me being so observant, I noticed several other women eyeballing as I gave him my number. More so, I wasn't sure if they were looking out of hate or were they interested in him too. I think they wanted him, so now I would make it my duty to see why they wanted him, while he wanted me. Hmmmm.

Before I could get to my car my
phone was ringing. "Hello"

"Aye what's up?"

The voice was sexy but I didn't
recognize it, so I replied, "Nothing, who is
this?"

"This is Brian from the parking lot a
few minutes ago. I decided to not wait until
tomorrow to call you. Me and my guys are
headed to Denny's and I was wondering if I
could treat you to an early breakfast."

"I appreciate the offer, but I'm good."

He immediately asked, "Oh, you have
a man or something?"

No, not at all, but I'm sure your
girlfriend wouldn't appreciate you out to
breakfast with me at 3 a.m."

"Real funny," he sighed, "Actually I
just got out of a four-year relationship like

six months ago. I am so damn single I should change my name to the ONE!!"

Man, I busted out laughing. "Seriously I'm drunk and I'm going home to give my pillow some head."

"Text me your address woman."

"Goodnight babe," and I hung up the phone even though I heard him still talking. I dreamed about Mr. Brian the passenger all that night. From the day I gave him my number we talked like 20 times a week and saw each other about once a month for a whole year without ever having sex. Brian was a different type of man, one I can't seem to explain or comprehend. He had a job, never had his own vehicle, lived with his parents, served in the military, was always horny, and always offering to show me his tongue skills.

Now word around town was that he offered his tongue to a lot of women. I have never been one to listen to rumors, so I disregarded all of that. More so, because I have heard so many rumors about myself that weren't true, which forces me to allow everyone to show and prove. If I didn't see it, I don't believe it 99.9% of the time. Plus, he seemed different. I mean, every time we met up he hugged and kissed me as if he cherished our every moment.

One night, I needed a shoulder to cry on and he was there for me. He picked me up in his dad's Dodge Durango and we rode around drinking Remy VSOP and talked for hours. By the end of the night, I honestly did not want him to leave. He made me feel so comfortable in his presence.

We arrived back at my apartment later that night and I invited him in. I told him to wait in the living room because I was so stressed that I wanted to take a hot shower to relax my body. He asked if I needed any help. I stated, "No, but I wouldn't mind your company." I went to turn the water on and then stepped away from the bathroom long enough to grab my cell phone and speaker. I placed them both on the counter and set it to my slow jam playlist. The first song to play was Marques Houston, "Naked". I put my hair into a ponytail and quickly removed my clothing. As I entered the shower, I was immediately aroused. He must have taken his clothes off in the room because nothing in the bathroom indicated that he had already got into the shower first.

The water was glistening off his body and it was a sight to see. However, it had been a long and exhausting day so I really did want to bathe. I nudged him out of the way by pushing my butt up against his thighs, close to his penis but not directly on it, just a little tease. I wanted to be in front so he could watch as I lathered up the soap on my curvaceous body, and that's what he did. He only watched for a little while and then washed himself. Ironically, we finished washing at the same time and in the back of my mind I was wondering if we could finish at the same time later on that night! (wink) We all have a freaky side. I'm just choosing to share my story…Anyways…

He must have been thinking the same things because as I reached over him to place my towel on the rack, he put me in a trance that was going to be very hard for me to break. Slightly he pushed my back up against the cold tile which sent a chill through my body causing my nipples to point directly to his attention. "I'm cold," I whispered.

Somehow the water was no longer hitting my body.

"Let me warm you up," he said.

He moved us closer by hugging me and taking baby steps into the water. While hugging me, he kept trying to kiss me on my lips and I tossed and turned my head repeatedly so that he was unsuccessful. Eventually I gave in and put out that night. One kiss had my heart pumping and my hips gyrating. I was in total disbelief. I'm not sure if the rumors were true that he goes around eating pussy, but what I do know is that his tongue game is WICKED!! Brian placed my left leg and then my right leg on his shoulders, lifted me up in the air and devoured the pussy. The shower felt like holy water, the pleasure was a blessing, and all I could say was, "Oh my God!" I'm not lying. I placed both hands on the back of his head and rolled my hips slowly, as if I was painting a picture with my body on his face. A pure work of art, I swear.

I came until I couldn't cum anymore. Already thrown back by him going in head first, I didn't even discourage him from quickly jumping into my pool of love with no life jacket, nor did I fear the consequences of our spur of the moment actions. This just wasn't my M.O.

That whole entire situation was so wrong, but it felt oh so good. It then dawned on me why females wanted him. We switched positions about five times. He came twice and damn near passed out going for the third. Between orgasms he went back to licking and playing with the pussy. Literally slurping up everything and moaning throughout the whole ordeal. Nasty, but I liked it.

27

C.T.

I loved every minute of ecstasy that his freaky ass gave. Any sexually dirty thing you can think of he did, and I let him do it too, TWICE. Whewww! After our first interaction we began to fool around like every two weeks. Between visits I wasn't sleeping with anyone else, but I knew he was and it began to bother me. Now don't get me wrong, there were always sexy men calling my phone, but I continued to turn them down because my mind was somewhere else. Basically, I fell in love with a man who only liked me.

One night after losing all inhibitions during a sexual episode, I asked, "Can I have you?"

He said, "You have me right here and right now."

"But I don't want to share you anymore. Don't you feel as though you are getting too old to be sleeping around?" He tried to soften the blow by telling me how good the sex was but in a nutshell, he denied my request, and his visits became sporadic. There was no speaking between sessions and episodes panned out to about once a month. Although when that time came once a month, he hugged, fucked, and kissed me as if we never missed a beat. This was mind-boggling. Maybe he was just a good lover with good dick and I was just wanting more than what was being offered. This sounded like a logical explanation in my mind because I knew that I wanted more than just sex. He began as a friend and then started to act as if I barely existed. I mean, I sent at least eight texts messages a week and he might've respond to one or none.

Eventually, none of my texts were sex-related. They may have said things like,

29

"hi", "good morning", or "how are you?" If nothing else, I wanted my friend back, and if possible, that dick too, but it wasn't mandatory, wanted but not needed. To make matters even worse he played me in so many ways. Randomly he would text and say he would be over for dinner at seven or something, and I would prepare a meal, put on something sexy, and have a wonderful night planned, to only eat by myself, tossing the leftovers and taking pictures of myself looking good. (Once again don't judge me; you all have done it before too).

Honestly, sometimes I would invite Foxy over to eat with me (when he stood me up) and we would just kick it and talk about life. There was two or three times where she said, "I know somebody must have stood you up because I know you aren't looking this good to be eating dinner with me"! Only once did I admit that there were unexpected changes in my plans, but the rest of the times I denied being stood up. Furthermore, I either claimed that I had a meeting or a prior engagement. She knew me too well, so she wasn't falling for it but never pressed the issue. One of the many reasons why I love her.

Sometimes, I would see Brian in the clubs and he would be all over me just to make other dudes jealous but at the same time keep them away from me. Brian was rare. Truthfully, he could have easily exposed me to any or everyone. I had sent numerous messages, made a lot of unanswered calls, and spent hours thinking of someone who could not care less. Confusingly, Brian would call when something personal was happening in his life and needed a confidant, but right after whatever situation he would go right back to the cold shoulder. Of course, I answered and always provided a shoulder to lie on, along with extending an open invitation into my life. Sometimes the actions were mutual. I could call him and say that my grandmother passed away and I needed someone to talk to and he would just appear like my guardian angel. Crazy right? So, I can't say he didn't care at all, but he sure had a strange way of showing it!

Maybe I am too bossy or too cocky. Maybe he was intimidated by my success. I don't know and I might never know. What I know is that I couldn't figure out why I wanted him so bad. Fuck, he had nothing to offer but his companionship. In the end I can't say that my feelings changed, but I had to be smart enough to understand there were plenty of other men who wanted me and he was not the last man on earth. One day he may come to his senses, but I may not be there with open arms.

Chapter 4 - Reflecting

Now yes, my BFFs were there any time I needed them, but I didn't always let them in on every aspect of my relationship or friendships with the opposite sex. It is often difficult for me to just express my emotions. Plus, people are so judgmental, and maybe it is or isn't intentional, but I don't like having to explain myself. Honestly, I don't like to see people shying away from a person they love because of other's opinions. Then you become secretive and no longer wanting to come around that judgmental person with the person you are dating, etc. The whole situation just turns into some bull, so I usually share information, but my deepest thoughts and attractions are usually not disclosed. I digress.

Call me crazy, but I really have moments where I have to sit down and evaluate my thoughts. Sometimes I have to force myself not to think too much about someone or a particular situation. It's kind of funny that most women are looking for a man who's genuinely interested in her and not just her body, but, if he brings up sex immediately after meeting then we assume that he is all about the physical. A lot of women would be like, "Girl he just wants to get some." However, we will know that same day of meeting a man if we would have sex with him, and possibly fantasized within the moment. We have to be honest with ourselves first before we can go trying to be honest and open-hearted with others. No one really wants to be alone, but on the other hand no one wants to be hurt, cheated on, lied to, or unappreciated. Nowadays, in my opinion, monogamy and marriage aren't highly valued.

See little do my friends know, I can imagine being with a man for a long time if we have a good connection on day one of meeting. Some people would tell me I'm crazy, but hey I'm just being honest. The downside to this is that you have created such high expectations that when things fall apart you are devastated and mad at the world. If you are a person like me, then you have to slow down.

Not every man you date will love you, like you, or desire you as you desire them, and it is ok. I promise there are so many men in this world and when you least expect it, the right one will find you. I was rambling for a moment, but you know I hit some key points. Anyways, I need to live more and stop overthinking.

Chapter 5 - D Boi

Damn, I feel like I forgot something. Oh well. I turned my head back, looked at the long line and decided I would have to get whatever it was another day and time. As I turned around I caught a glimpse of the cutie standing directly behind me. He stood about 6ft tall, caramel skin complexion, with a crispy haircut, and a freshly groomed face. He was rocking a fresh pair of Cazals that definitely caught my eye, stonewashed True Religion jeans, a chocolate pair of Cole Haan's, with a matching pea coat. Everything about him said, "D-Boi" (Dope Dealer), which normally doesn't turn me on, but it was something about him.

My hair was done but I only had on some pink polo sweats, some shades, my jacket, and some cute boots. Obviously, I wasn't at my best and he was still checking me out. After scanning all of my groceries, I reached in my purse to pay and he immediately stepped up and said, "Let me take care of this for you."

With a look of disbelief, I replied, "Are you sure you can afford to pay for mine and yours?"

He laughed and said, "Once you get to know me, you'll find out that you should have never asked me a question like that." By the way his eyebrows narrowed down while keeping a smile on his face, I could tell he felt a little insulted and turned on at the same time.

"Well thank you very much Mr...?"

"Dave."

"Dave what?"

"Dave Harris."

"Well thank you Mr. Harris."

"You are very welcome Ms. Lovelace."

"Hmmm, so you read my badge huh?"

"Yes I did," he said.

I walked off switching my hips from left to right. By the time I got to my car, he had come right up behind me and began grabbing bags to help put into the trunk, WOW!! "Are you a stalker?" I asked.

"Hell NO, Mrs. Lady, every beautiful woman deserves a strong man to help take the weight off her hands every now and then."

"Oh, so the ugly chicks are screwed?"

"Cute and funny, ummmhmmm," he said. "Were you really going to leave without giving a brother your number?"

"You didn't ask me for my number did you?"

"May I have your number please?"

"Sure, its 313-555-5555 and once again thank you."

"No problem, I will hit you up later."

I went home put my groceries up and then spread out across my California King Bed. It had been another long day in the office, plus it was a Saturday. I was so tired of having to put in those extra hours on Saturdays. It didn't happen too often, but when it did, it would drain me. People often have the misconception that working for the radio station HOT 107.1 in the advertising department means all fun and games. NOT!! I had to play the background for 2 years before I started seeing the perks. My job consists of a lot of hours of paperwork, networking, phone calls, and constant emails with reminders of the multiple deadlines. Sometimes it is overwhelming, but there are sooo many perks that come along with the job, so I don't complain too often.

I quickly gave Mr. Harris the nickname of D-Boi for two reasons: First of all, his name is Dave. Two, I believed that he either sold drugs or had rich parents, but 9 times of 10 he probably sold dope. It could have been the fact that I knew he would spend whatever on me. I don't know, but so far so good and this was day one.

This man did require a chat with my bffs, so I hopped on a video chat with Foxy and Michele. I told them all about my quick few minutes with Dave. They were genuinely happy for me as if I was already dating him. Michele said that I should try to be a little reserved. I think that she was implying that I am too ready to jump into a relationship. I was like ok ok ok, good advice. Now Foxy agreed with Michele but was saying stuff like, "Pay attention to how he dresses, speaks, how much he tips if y'all go out, etc." I laughed because both of them swear that they are relationship experts but I valued both of their opinions.

Riding down I-94, the Wednesday after I met Dave, I realized that 96 hours had gone by and he didn't call my phone, not one time. When I got home I turned on the Ready album by Trey Songz, lit two sea salt scented candles, and ran some bath water so I could relax. I slipped out of my clothes and just stared at my naked body in the mirror. I don't know about other women, but I love my body. Nice booty, little gut, thick thighs, and breast that turned me on by just looking at them. Thoughts of Dave standing behind me with one hand between my legs and his lips on my neck repeatedly played as I gazed into the mirror. I shook my head a few times, turned around, and slowly stepped into my heart shaped tub.

The water felt great, so I laid back and let the tub have all of me. After a while, I sat up washed, relaxed more, and then my phone rang. "Hello," I whispered.

"Are you sleeping?"

"No, I'm in the tub."

"It's been a few days, what time should I pick you up?"

"I thought you forgot."

"I wouldn't dare. What would make you say that?"

"Hmmm, you haven't called since I met you."

He snickered and then stated, "In my line of work, I make a lot of moves and I hate being interrupted. Just know that when I have time, I would love to spend some with you and I have time tonight."

43

I said, "What if I'm busy tonight, will
there be a second chance?"

He laughed, "So are you available?"

"Actually, I'm not in the mood for
going out, but I would love to have you
over." He was ok with it, so I told him the
address and to be here around 8pm. He
arrived on time with a comfy looking grey
polo sweat suit and a pair of Jordan slippers.
I laughed in my head because I felt like he
was trying to make himself at home. Now let
me inform you real quick, I was skeptical
after making our first date in my home, but I
was really tired and interested, so I took a
chance. He had two bags in his hand as he
was approaching my door. (Yeah I saw all
this from the window, but what I didn't see
was the car he drove). The doorbell rang and
I waited a few seconds as if I was walking to

the door. I opened the door and he smiled shyly as I escorted him into the living room.

Immediately he set his bags on the coffee table and asked for a hug, I leaned in and he whispered, "You look good and smell good too."

I said thank you and complimented his soft Polo sweater.

"I got sushi for takeout and a bottle of Moscato."

My eyebrows rose out of curiosity because I had never tried sushi and because I couldn't believe that he chose this as our meal. I went into the kitchen to grab plates and glasses. When I returned, he already found the remote and had the Pistons vs Cavaliers game going. Plus, his cell phone was charging in the outlet and his slippers were off. Sarcastically I asked, "Are you comfortable?"

He asked if I ever had sushi and I said, "No." So he pulled out the chopsticks, grabbed a piece, and fed it to me. To my surprise it was delicious. I ate a whole roll as we watched the game and just talked about sports. Dave was impressed with my knowledge of sports and I was just as impressed with him in general.

Throughout the game his phone rang a few times, but he ignored it. The final score was Detroit 119 to Cavs 118. He said he had $700 on the game and needed to go pick up his money before dudes got to acting funny. Dave helped me clean up our mess and I walked him to the door. He left me with the softest kiss on my lips and one on my cheek, I'm not exaggerating! It was about 11pm, he said I'll call you tonight and I said ok.

We talked on the phone that night and a few more nights before our next date. Our

next date was at a billiards place where we
shot pool, laughed, and drank all night. I had
a blast and he was super funny and sexy, but
we both decided that the next date needed to
be something more official. You know, like a
fancy restaurant, play, or something. The
next date didn't come for another two to
three weeks after the second. However, in
between time, he was texting, sending
flowers to my job, and randomly leaving
notes on my car. It sounds kind of like a
stalker to some, but they were cute gestures
to me.

Eventually he called one night, "What
are you doing? I haven't seen you in so
long."

"Nothing, in the tub, I was starting to
think that you just wanted to be my texting or
phone buddy.

"Girl stop teasing me," he joked,
"Can I pick you up at 8?"

"I'm always down to see you," was
my response.

"What are you wearing tonight?"

"What would you like me to wear?
Anything you can think of I can
accommodate because I love clothes."

"How about something brown," he
said.

"Alright, I have a tan dress with a
gold necklace and brown knee-high boots, to
match?"

"Sounds sexy, but what do you have
on now?"

"I'm in the tub, and you are a man, so
trust me when I say I expected that question."

"Well damn, I will see you shortly
beautiful."

Undeniably, I was impressed. At 8pm he was parked outside my condo in a pearl blue Camaro on 24-inch rims and the sounds were banging. He stood outside holding the passenger door open wearing a tan sweater, brown jeans, and a pair of tan Gator boots. For a D Boi, he cleaned up nicely and he coordinated with me on purpose. That was a cute gesture.

Even though we both could hear his phone ringing in his pocket, he held complete eye contact with me as I walked out of my door and into his arms. He hugged me and whispered in my ear, "You look great," and then ushered me into the car. This guy even put my seatbelt on for me. I'm not sure if he had on Axe Body Spray or not, but just like the commercial, once I took a whiff, I was ready to be all over him. But I kept my cool…whew…he didn't know how close I came to be giving that car a good show.

He closed my door and then walked behind the car and had about a three-minute conversation with someone on the phone. "Sorry about that babe," he stated, once he finally got into the car. "If it's okay with you I need to make one quick stop to pick up some money."

"No problem, sir, as long as you agree to never have me involved in any illegal or dangerous situations."

"Agreed," he said, and I trusted him.

He made his move and we were just cruising because I had no idea where we were going. Out of the blue, he turns the music down and says, "Could you see yourself being with someone like me?"

"I don't know yet, slow down big fella," I said jokingly.

"But I'm living a fast life my baby. I'm making fast money, driving fast cars, and I follow my instincts."

"Right now I'm feeling you."

"Alright, alright, alright, how about we discuss this a little more over dinner?"

I nodded my head in agreement. We pulled up to a restaurant I had only heard rumors about. Star Studded was the name. It was absolutely beautiful. As we entered the building with these marvelous glass doors we stopped at the greeter and she asked for our names. He stated Lovelace. "We have a wonderful night planned for you two, so let me lead you to the rooftop. I followed behind the greeter and he followed behind me, so I made sure that I gave a little more jiggle with each step because I knew he was watching.

The greeter led us to an elevator that took us up to the rooftop. Very, very, very, exquisite taste this man had. He could have just taken me to Red Lobster. The rooftop was divided into eight sections that provided complete isolation and privacy for each party, but also provided a brilliant view of Detroit.

"So are you enjoying our first actual date?" he asked

"Well I enjoyed our blind date at the grocery store and all of the times before this babe."

"Oh yeah, all of that was straight too, but this is what I would have in mind when I ask a beautiful woman like yourself if she wants to step out with me."

Our conversation was interrupted by a beautiful Brazilian looking female waitress carrying a tray with a champagne bottle and two glasses. "To start the evening while you all look over the menu, I have a bottle of our finest champagne the restaurant has to offer," she stated.

We both said, "thank you," as she poured, and he gave her a $5 tip.

"So let's play 21 questions," he said with a sense of urgency.

I laughed and said, "Let me look over the menu first, damn babe."

"How about you let me order for you," he said.

I didn't mind so I said, "Go ahead, the night belongs to you.". As I glanced over the menu, I saw nothing under $54.99, so I didn't know what to order without being expensive or greedy. Bottom line is that I'm glad he offered to order for me. "Let me go first sir, do you have a girlfriend, wife, or steady sex partner? I know I've asked this before but things may have changed since I first met you."

He said, "No, no, and not really."

"Now my turn, you answer all of those same questions you asked me and tell me whether or not you want any of those 3 options that you don't have already."

Sincerely, I replied with, "No, no, and I want good company, everything else will come naturally."

I caught him off guard with my last, and he was like, "Damn, good answer," but you could tell that it wasn't the one he was looking for.

"Okay, so when I told you that I live a fast life, can you see yourself doing the same in the moments that we are together?"

"I believe I can," I stated. The waiter came back and he ordered us two medium well steaks, loaded baked potatoes, jumbo black tiger shrimps, and Caesar salads. His choice of dinner sounded delicious.

"Back to what I was talking about," he said.

"Umm, I'm listening," I stated while taking a sip from my glass.

He said, "What if I asked for a kiss right now?"

"My only reply is that you make sure I like it."

He got up from his seat, grabbed me by my hand and led me to the window. Dave placed both of my arms around his shoulders; his left hand was on my waist, and he used his right hand to lift my chin and kissed me with a bit of eagerness and passion. Naturally I was aroused and he knew it. The kiss probably only lasted for five seconds but it felt like a half hour. Once he released my lips, my eyes were still closed as if I was hypnotized. He slid behind me and we looked out over the city. We quickly shared our thoughts about each other while anticipating our meal and how the night may end...Well I don't know about him, but the end of the night was on my mind.

Initially after that kiss I wanted to have him ask for some to go boxes, but I didn't want to rush things or look easy. See, we have thoughts like men occasionally; however, we are smart enough to not always act upon those thoughts. I can't always say the same about guys.

Once the waitress returned with the food, my mind had changed! The steaks smelled great and the whole presentation was very attractive. "Enjoy," the waitress stated as she placed our meals in front of us.

We both said, "Thanks," and he handed her a $20 tip this time. I think it was because of the way she licked her lips as she was walking away the last time, when he handed her the $5. I wasn't mad because she was pretty and even I had to do a double take, but then I thought like forget that bitch, I was eating, and she was serving hahahahahaha.

Before I could touch my silverware he grabbed my hand and said, "Bow your head." This sexy ass, dope dealing man, was a God-fearing man too??? I couldn't believe it. We didn't pray before the sushi or the little bar foods we had shared previously. He gave grace and we said, "Amen." In the back of my mind, I was thinking, *"Who was this, the devil in disguise?"* I knew he worked for Comcast, but he couldn't afford this lifestyle on his salary, so he must have been doing something. Unfortunately, I never asked.

We talked and ate our delicious meals together. His conversation was great. Dave gave many compliments, we discussed my job, his job, and our past relationships, goals, etc. and then he suggested we take our dessert to go. I agreed. Soon as the waitress came back we let her know we wanted boxes, she quickly disappeared and returned with everything ready to go. Surprisingly, he tipped the waitress again by leaving a $20 on the table along with the bill. We excused ourselves and headed to the car. Once he got in, after ushering me into the car, he asked for a kiss again. This time I advised him to live in the moment; body language will determine whether it is or is not okay to kiss me, and I was in the middle of my sentence when he leaned across the center console, turned my face towards him, and kissed me with less eagerness and more passion! OMG, you would have thought he went to school and learned how to treat a woman.

That V8 engine did about 100mph down the highway. He kept his left hand on the steering wheel and his right hand on my left thigh. The way he moved his hand up and down my leg was turning me on. That tingling sensation went down to my feet and up to my breast, but he hadn't touched either place. What an amazing feeling he gave me. I licked my bottom lip, exhaled, and continued to bob my head to the music. I was trying my hardest to give off the false impression that the grip and touch of his warm hands were not affecting me.

Slowly he removed his hand from my thigh to place both hands on the steering wheel, so he could control his car while getting off on the downtown exit. Typical male move right here, he says, "If I can come in and have a drink with you I will stop at the store. (men will usually say something similar to this, basically trying to ask to come over for a drink.)

"I have everything you can think of,"
I said, "No need to stop."

"Do you have whipped cream?"

"Yes."

"Ice?"

"Yes."

With a bright smile, he asked, "Baby
oil?"

"Yes, but I'm not sure you will need
this stuff babe."

In a mannish tone he said, "I'm a
giver and you will find that out sooner than
later.

There was no response needed, so I
said nothing. He pulled up to my condo and
parked right in front of my door. He grabbed
the dessert from the backseat, which was like
several containers, and I didn't know why
and I didn't ask. He made his way to the
passenger side, opened my door, and I

stepped out. Once we reached my door he pulled me by my waist closer to him and kissed me as if he was leaving.

I said, "Are you leaving me to eat all of this dessert alone?"

"No, why would say that?"

"Never mind," I said.

We entered my home and took our shoes off at the door. I led him into the living and asked to take his jacket. He hands me his jacket and snatches up the remote, quick, fast, and in a hurry and then looked at me and asked, "Can I see Sports Center real quick?"

"Help yourself, I need to put this stuff in the closet and freshen up in the bathroom." As I came back into the room, he had the desserts spread across the table. There were strawberries, ice cream, two large slices of chocolate cake, and it looked delicious, just like our entrée earlier. Actually, he looked good too, and he had this look in his eyes like he could eat me for dessert and forget all about that damn cake. I know I'm a freak but shhh don't tell anybody.

"You have some very sexy lips."

"Thank you sir," I said, as he fed me a slice of chocolate cake. A piece of frosting got on the corner of my mouth, I licked my lips but didn't get it all, so he instantly jumped on the opportunity to softly lick the remaining frosting off my face and then kissed me as softly as he had just licked my face. Mmm Mmm Mmm. Okay he just crossed the line and unknowingly had entered a sexual paradise.

His phone rang but he ignored it and kept all of his attention on me, while whispering in my ear, "Am I moving too fast for you?"

"Body language babe!" He had a hard time deciding when the right time to make a move was. All he had to do was go with the flow until it felt wrong and then ask questions. You know what I'm saying?

"I do have a couple more questions," he said while laughing and taking in deep breaths.

With eyebrows raised, I said, "Yes!"

Do you mind if I take off this shirt and these pants and make us some drinks? Oh, and I have basketball shorts on under my jeans, I'm not trying to get naked but I want to get comfortable.

"Make yourself comfortable," I said but mumbled get naked if you would like. "No offense Dave, but I have a pet peeve for not allowing others to make my drink, so I can pour my own troubles."

As he undressed, I couldn't help but keep glancing at his man print in the front of those shorts. I know I know I know, I must have a damn fetish for sexy men in gym shorts, but I am not ashamed. I grabbed a little ice, poured a little Remy, and just sat back. He rubbed my thighs while fumbling around with his phone. Little did he know, my hormones were elevating and I was getting ready to become the aggressor!

Unbelievably, after a while, he interrupted my naughty thoughts by stating, "Well Ms. Lovelace, I have had a great time tonight and I hope this won't be the last time I see you."

"Only if you want it to be, and yes I did enjoy your company sir."

He attempted to stand up as if he was getting ready to leave and then asked if he could crash on the couch since he was drunk, and it was extremely late. I said, "Of course," and he plopped down on the couch hard and flat on his back as if lightning hit him. It was hilarious and disappointing all in one. I just shook my head and asked if he was okay.

The dude slapped his own face twice and said, "I can't fall asleep without a kiss goodnight."

Shockingly I couldn't believe that he couldn't see how ready I was. I was seriously thinking about taking matters into my own hands, if you know what I mean! In my moment of heat, he gently placed a peck on my lips and then asked me to come and lay with him on the couch, instead of going to the room alone.

I'm almost like a man; I hate being aroused for no reason. It's like a waste of my essence (the juices). Seriously, I'm not joking, and I know I'm not the only woman who feels this way.

Anyways, I slid right behind him on the couch. Lying on my side, I placed one leg between his legs and my left arm across his waist. He kissed me and said, "Goodnight," in a drunken slur, but slowly continued to kiss me as if he just realized that he liked kissing me. He slid his hands down my back, sliding his fingers right pass my ass to the essence of my love. Ouuuweee! Yes, your thoughts aren't deceiving you. I took my panties off when I went to the bathroom and freshened up… Anyways, once the juices ran down his fingertips he was wide awake and at attention. Literally and physically at full attention.

Gripping me by my thighs he pulled me right on top of him, it was on. I began to kiss every spot that looked good. I started with his lips, neck, chest, and then I reached down into his shorts pulling out this even toned thick, long, silky, sexy penis and began to place kisses on the head. No sucking, just tongue kissing the dick as if it was his lips. You have to keep him and his man's happy. Seduction is an art, not just an action in the heat of the moment, but I digress.

He moaned, while I worked my magic. If he didn't know, I love a man who moans, so what was once a small river turned into an ocean and I wanted him to ride the waves. All we needed was a little more foreplay and a life jacket.

"Damn, can I marry you?" he laughed. Sitting in a straddle position I sat up and removed my sweater and bra, then placed my D cups right in his face. "Your titties didn't look this big earlier."

"And now?" I asked in a seductive tone.

"No disrespect but they are big as hell and I am loving them!!"

Still in a straddle position he placed that diving board right in front of my swimming pool and I jumped on it. Splash! My impulse reaction had me acting without thinking but I'm glad he was 10 thoughts ahead of me. Safety first and I proceeded with caution. To make a long story short, the sex was good, his conversation was great, and everything was flowing smoothly. We spent 2 years of living in the fast lane. I can't lie, I didn't want for anything when I was with my D Boi. Do you hear me?

Seriously, he took me to every restaurant in the city you could think of. We took flights for the weekends, we hung out with his family and my family, we went to church together, we fucked on my balcony, spent a lot of money with the Purple Rose Clothing label out of ATL, and we made love in my bed and his bed, etc. Often, he would send flowers to the radio station with a note that only stated, "I was thinking of you". I wasn't in love with him because of his money. It was because he took the time out of his life to spend with me, and I love a man who loves to be in my presence. It was to the point where he was calling Foxy and Michele sis and they called him bro! I was in DEEP! But I'm not sure if all of our good days can outweigh our last day together.

It was something odd about his behavior. He kept asking questions like, what if this happened or what if that happened? You know when someone is acting differently. As we laid on the couch where we often shared intimate conversations, I could barely keep my eyes open. I was sexually drained, tired from work, and just a whole bunch of other stuff, but he kept trying to hold a conversation. So, I sat up and looked him dead in his face and asked, "Babe is there something you need to tell me?"

He said, "No," kissed me and lowered me back down to the couch.

Something wasn't right, so in a sterner voice I said, "Something isn't right," and I sat up again, but stared at him even harder. Suspiciously he rubbed his head like he was confused or scared to say something. Keeping my eyes on him, I laid back and positioned myself where we were facing each other. "Move your hand," I said, as I caressed his head and let my hand sail through his deep waves he so loved to brag about. My intent was to assure him he had my full attention and empathy. His breathing became rapid, but he still wouldn't say a word. He said, "I'm damn near wanting to cry right now telling you about this". Literally I was scared. Somehow I felt as though my life was in danger and was becoming terrified.

My eyes were beginning to water. I know he could hear the tone of fear, suspicion, and concern in my voice, but yet I was asking him, "Is your life or our lives in danger?" Before he could answer I'm like, "Whatever it is can you assure me that nobody knows anything about me, where I live or whatever?"

First he said, "Yea," and then said, "I don't know." Then he stated, "You are too smart for your own good." Unexpectedly he had a moment of honesty and I could do nothing but listen. "You are the best thing that has ever happened to a man like me, I have only slept with one other woman since the first time we slept together, and I LOVE YOU. I have never told another woman this before and actually meant it. Truthfully, I'm getting ready to get locked up and I have never been to prison, I'm on the run and I am nervous, and this and that and so on and so forth…"

People could have come in and robbed me of everything and I would not have moved an inch. I WAS STUCK IN TOTAL DISBELIEF, BUT MORE BECAUSE I WAS YOUNG AND NAÏVE. Physically my legs felt glued to the sofa and my heart felt buried under the lies and the idea that I was so naïve or such an idiot to have given my heart to a man like him. I cried, cried, cried, and could have drowned in my tears. We spoke no words to each other for about an hour. My jaw kept clenching and the tears kept flowing. He just kept wiping my face and kissing me and saying, "I love you".

In my wildest imagination, I couldn't have experienced a nightmare that would compare to what happened that night. While I stared at the wall trying to think to myself about how much time we had left, what if we got pulled over and he went to jail, or what if they kicked in my fucking door. I must have hit the nail on its damn head, the irony was horrific. BANG, BANG, BANG!!! Three hard knocks on the door quickly broke the bond between me and the sofa. I headed straight for the door and he stopped me in my tracks telling me to hold on and handed me about 30 rolls of $100 bills, almost the size of a cigarette. "There's like a grand in each roll. Give 10 to my mom and you can have the rest, just look out for me while I'm in there.

"Open up, it's the police!" the officer shouted.

I took the money and hid them in the first discrete place that came to mind, which was inside a box with some panty liners and sanitary napkins in the bathroom closet. He came in behind me and kissed me with tears in his eyes.

I said, "I love you," and just looked at him in disbelief and disappointment. He kissed me again, apologized, took his sim card out of his phone, dropped it down the bathroom sink, turned the water on and left it running on the phone. He walked out into the living room and yelled, "Who are you looking for?"

"David Harris," the officer stated.

"We have the place surrounded and you have to the count of 10 to open the door or we'll kick it in," another officer demanded.

LIKE. LUST. LOVE

I watched from the sofa as he slowly
unlocked the front door, ran back towards the
kitchen and yelled, "ITS UNLOCKED!"
About ten officers entered my condo with
guns and a canine. They had me lay flat on
the ground as they terrorized my entire home.
I wasn't worried about too much because I
knew there were no drugs there, so I just
wanted them to do their search and hurry up
and leave. After being read his rights, two
officers escorted Dave out of my life!

To my surprise they didn't find the
money, nor did they take me, but what they
did do was fuck my crib up, and I had to put
it all back together. The next day I took the
money over to his mother's house and we
cried together. She was disappointed in his
actions and informed me that she had
encouraged him several times to leave me
alone, so he wouldn't break my heart by

C.T.

getting locked up or killed out in the streets.
Like a man living in the fast lane, he was
moving too quickly to listen, but I appreciate
all the time we spent together and the love we
shared; but sometimes I think that we should
have remained strangers.

Chapter 6 - I Give Up

By this time, I'm now 25 years old and single. Going to work and home every day made me think about how much I missed Dave, but I couldn't believe that I had fallen in love with a criminal. The story was all over the news and every social media outlet. I had introduced this man to my friends, family members, coworkers, etc. He had introduced me to his friends, family members, and coworkers…*shaking my head*… Honestly, I was embarrassed and naïve all in one. Once again, the signs were there but yet I ignored them, so shame on me.

On the other hand, things were so good I couldn't leave or slap some sense into myself. My past boyfriends or partners were good dudes with good dick, but he had me feeling some type of way. It was like we were in a world of our own, a whole other league. I can't explain it, but I had to see where it would have taken me, and I have no regrets.

After Dave got locked up, I decided to not date for a while. Of course I was still looking out for him while he was locked up, accepting phone calls, with a few visits here and there, but I wasn't committed to him or anyone else. I damn near wanted to run a complete background check on dudes, along with a lie detector test. Just to be on the safe side, you know. I had let a whole year and three months go by without getting slow stroked or ate for dinner. I know I'm talkin' dirty because that's how I am feeling. There is nothing like sending your man that "come and get it" text and he's knocking at the door in 20 mins to knock you down for 30 mins and then be knocked out for 90 minutes. I'm due!!!

To accomplish my goal of getting knocked off, I played the field a little bit. So, let me give you all a quick summary of how the next four to five months went. (19-20 months no Dave)

First off, I started by frequently hitting bars after work. I was in there for no more than 45 minutes to see if anyone caught my eye, and if they did I gave them my number just to see where it could take me. I have never in my life met a man so fine I had to take him home the same night I met him and give up the goodies.

After being single for a while I decided to walk on the other side of the tracks. Occasionally my friends and I used to joke about dating a white guy, but there was actually one who caught my eye. His name was Nathaniel Groot, so I just called him G. He worked for the corporate office downtown for AT&T. This guy was very standout-ish. Unfortunately, he was shorter than me, younger than me, and white. Obviously he had two strikes against him. However, he was persistent with trying to date me, very confident, super cool, with a sexy voice, swag, and a few dollars he was more than willing to share with me. Oh yeah and he loved to play poker. Damn, I love a man who plays poker ALMOST...ALMOST as much as I love a man in hoop shorts.

It started off with us talking on the phone once or twice a month. Then we had lunch on Thursdays and we would have very detailed and intimate conversations that rarely involved sex. One day we skipped lunch and met up for dinner, and once I saw him outside of his business attire...I was really attracted to him, but he would have never known because I remained cool. Randomly he would send text messages like, "Let me be your man and I promise I will treat you right." No doubt for the most part he had my attention, but I couldn't seem to get myself to go too far with him.

After a few months of lunch and dinner we hung out more often. At the same time he knew that we weren't exclusive and that with my particular job I may be invited to various parties and events where there may be temptations. To be honest we weren't sleeping together so I didn't know why I often felt the need to explain myself after flirting or going out with someone else. Even though he was sending flowers for no reason, buying me my favorite candy bar just to be nice and was genuinely a caring and giving person. Now some may say so what was the problem?

He lacked the ability to seduce me. Maybe he was so used to women throwing themselves at him that he never had to put forth any effort. The fact that he didn't possess this quality made it easier for me to not think about him sexually. It crossed my mind a few times. Especially one night when he called and said he was by my house and was wondering if he could borrow a CD. My first thought was that this guy will say anything to try and come over. Immediately, I told him that my hair wasn't done, and I wasn't coming outside but I would put it in the mailbox. He was all like damn I can't see you. I said, no. So when he pulls up he asked for a specific CD in the car, so I hit the unlock button and watched him as he grabbed the CD and suspiciously placed a bag in there too.

I called him like what was that you put in my car and his response was go see. I assumed that it was probably an Arizona Iced Tea and that if I left it there overnight that it would still be cold in the morning, but he insisted that I could put a scarf on my head and run out to the car. After he begged me a few times to go outside and assured me I wouldn't be disappointed, I put on some sweats, my bonnet, and some flip flops and went out to the car. I looked inside and as I guessed there was a tall can of Arizona Tea but surprisingly on the passenger seat there was a bag of Hershey kisses.

"You ruined my great idea," he said.

"How so?" I said with much curiosity.

"Because, I was going to give them to you and then ask if I could have one, and once you said yes I was going to pull you close and kiss you softly on those sexy ass lips...but it's over now. Enjoy." And he hung up the phone. I admired his creativity and I felt a little bad. I just couldn't DO IT.

After Nate, I hung out with a few more guys but none really had my undivided attention. Out of those few guys, I only slept with one and it was more so because I was too far past due. He just caught me on a good night and he got lucky. It wasn't a one-night stand because I had known him for a while, but he most certainly did nothing to deserve it.

Chapter 7 - Look No Further

There have been plenty of times that a random cutie has caught my attention, whether it was at a game, job event, or like before at the freakin' grocery store. But there was this one time that things were different because something about him was different.

I was in New York for a grand opening for a new station. It was basically a live recording and a little photo Op with guest hosts and/or members of other stations and he was filming the event. I moved around the venue throughout the night and he still continued to catch my eye on numerous occasions. I noticed him but I wasn't in the mood for going beyond my job duties. Honestly, I didn't want to be there because my nephew Tommie had just passed away down in Arkansas and I was still in my feelings... Right before the event ended, they had switched cameramen and he was in the crowd mingling. Eventually he made his way to me and introduced himself as Jakari Taylor.

His follow up line stated something about how he couldn't help but notice me looking down and out throughout the night. He asked if I was single, I said yes, gave him my number and we talked on the phone for hours that night. I felt so good and comfortable while speaking with him. He is such a great listener. Since that night, I haven't gone a night without speaking to him.

Jakari initiated every conversation by asking me how was my day? Our conversations were so much more than I was used to. We would discuss things like traveling, credit, goals, sex, education, and views on relationships. Let me not forget to mention that his voice really does something to me. He literally turns me on ALL OF THE TIME.

After several months of talking and racking up frequent flyer miles, he calls out the blue and says that he was moving to Detroit. I felt like it was too good to be true. I couldn't wait to have all of him next to me more often. At the time Jakari was 26 years old, 6ft 3in and 180lbs with dark brown skin, the color of a Hershey bar, brown sugar colored eyes, and soft wavy hair. I love rubbing my fingers thru his hair while we lay and watch movies, or while he's pleasing me.

You know how things may be going just fine the way they were but then one change can throw things off. However, that wasn't the case this time!! Things continued to go smoothly. He moved out towards Canton like 20 minutes away from me, so it was all good until we began going out more frequently and attending numerous events together. Shockingly I was insecure. More so because he wasn't very confident, but very sexy and too many women were throwing themselves at him. I must admit I was a little on edge. But every and anytime he kissed me, I would fall in love over and over again!

Being that I am such an over thinker, I sometimes questioned whether or not I was deserving of such a well put together man. I wouldn't dare tell you that he's perfect, but he's perfect for ME! I have plenty of stories about how women are physically and/or emotionally abused in their relationships, but I have experienced none of this with Jakari. And our relationship isn't perfect at all. We have our small arguments about simple stuff like other couples. Jakari is always complaining about a compliment that someone gave me on social media, that's one of his biggest problems, but that's his own insecurities. I just try to remind him that I'm with him, and that I share my home with him, lie down with him every night. He's the only man that I love and make love to, so the comments online are cool but being with him is even greater. I'm usually quick to fuss about him not cleaning up behind himself, not keeping enough gas in the cars, or hell, we might even argue about him cummin' quickly, when I want to go all night. No matter what, he keeps it 100 at all times. He can be brutally honest, but so can I!

One day we were talking about the role and responsibility of a husband. I was able to start off with two or three sentences before he cut me off and said "stop right there". He said these next words, almost verbatim, "As a husband it is my responsibility to be her provider, lover, protector, confidant, back bone, chef, porn star etc., but I can't lose myself while trying to be all of those things. Y'all women be wanting us to turn into blind yes men," and he laughed. "Females want you to do whatever, whenever, and pretty much ignore anybody or anything else in their lives. Women need to be more realistic and understand that if you continue to display all of the same qualities that made him present a ring, then your position will be secure in his life. But women will make a man do so much to maintain a good relationship." He ended his sermon (haha) with, "Meet us at the table and just remember that good sex and that pretty ring is not going to keep that man around.

As men, we know that if a woman was handling her business before we came into the picture (house, car, clothes, job, etc.) then we know that she could/can do the same without us, but that doesn't mean to keeping throwing it in our faces. He paused for a second and then said but you complete me, to whom much is given, much is required, and I love you babe because you are different; we are different."

I felt all of that! I'm not going to try and break it down for y'all because it's all about an understanding. What I understood may have been perceived differently from the next woman, but the message was clear to me. The way he thinks is just another reason why I love him.

Just yesterday, he came up with the idea that we should start blogging. Even though my role at the station isn't always in the eye of the public, I do have like 84K followers on IG, and he has like 176K followers, due to being so great with that camera. He's normally filming different events, independent films, interviews for the 3rd Coast Avenue Show on YouTube, and other things. He's also been doing photography a lot lately to make a bigger name for himself in the world. His idea was to start filming for the next few months and see how people respond to that. If we grew a large number of viewers, then we would keep it going.

At first I was a little concerned about our privacy being invaded, but he assured me that we would be fine, despite the fact that he was going to be randomly filming during random moments. He even joked about surprisingly popping up on me at random places. I laughed it off and told him I was ready. By the next day he was filming. Jakari would film while we were brushing our teeth, while I was walking to the car, while grocery shopping, right before sex (not during), while eating dinner, he would pop up at my job, film while at his job, etc. Our viewers went from 1k the first week to 9k by the end of the second month. It was crazy, but I was loving every minute and I was able to share countless lovable memories with the world.

***

Lord I thank you for waking me up this morning and protecting me all these years. I am blessed and grateful for your grace and mercy. I can't even lie, sometimes, I doubted you Lord, but I have come this far by faith. Some may say that it's crazy how people can go from smoking weed, drinking, and premarital sex to calling upon the name of the Almighty. It's true, I have been wasted, dealt with drug dealers, lied, and cheated.

However, God knows all, hears all, and sees all.

As I sat on the toilet listening to the bird's chirp outside of the window, I just kept thinking I was blessed. I was finally on my path to Endless Love Lane. I felt so spiritual, and no it was not a Sunday. Jakari had not proposed or even mentioned the word marriage but I knew on that day I prayed God blessed me to spend the rest of my days with this man. I was in love and it felt so good to even be thinking about it while doing something as simple as using the bathroom first thing in the morning...

My thoughts were interrupted by two soft knocks, followed by a pushy voice saying, "Hurry up and get dressed, I have something planned for us today" ... I hoped that he was just joking and when I opened the door, he would bend me over the edge of the bed and put me back to sleep if you know what I mean. Lord please forgive me.

Instead, he was clothed with the camera in my face and a look of anticipation and impatience on his face. Seriously, this man already had an outfit laid out for me, shoes, and all. So I hopped in the shower, got dressed and off we went. We headed down I-94 just cruising. It was about 69° outside, so the windows were cracked and the breeze felt great. After 15-20 minutes the car came to a stop and we were parked at a little privately-owned shop. The sign read, best brunch in town. I love to eat so I was excited, plus I love how he looks me in my eyes at the table while we eat. He makes me feel like we're on our first date every single time.

I ordered the breakfast jambalaya with shrimp, eggs, cheese, and veggies, minus the potatoes, and he had scrambled eggs with an 8oz steak. "Do you still think about your ex?"

First I looked at the camera, then looked back at him. He caught me off guard with the question, but my answer was, "No not really. We all sometimes reflect or reminisce about our past right?"

"I feel you," he said.

I then gave him that look like, what's up, where did that come from? Instantly I became defensive and said, "Is there something you want to tell me?" with a bitchy attitude.

He laughed and said, "Yes and no..." Oh Lord my mind went through a thousand scenarios in 8.7 seconds. "It's just that my ex has been trying to get at me tough."

I'm baffled because in my mind I'm thinking he took me to brunch to break up with me publicly just in case I flip out. "Did you tell her you have been involved with a woman for a year and a half?"

"YES," he said, "But she was like I see no ring on your finger."

"What the hell?!" I asked as my voice elevated to another octave. "Am I supposed to propose to you? Turn the damn camera off," I said sternly.

He laughed again, "Chill out girl. And no, she was just saying that because I proposed to her only to discover shortly after that she had still been sleeping with her ex."

I grabbed his hand and looked him right into his eyes and said, "I would never cheat on you, hell I'll never leave unless you absolutely force me too. I love you more than you know. And I don't cuss too often but FUCK her..."

"See, that's what I needed to hear baby, I love you too..." and then he busted out his own remix to a track by Tyrese, singing, "And one day Imma make you my wife/I was excited cause I keep falling, falling in love with youuu." Jakari turned off the camera and we finished eating breakfast.

He could tell by the look in my eyes I was turned on by our love confessions, so he paid for the bill and we headed to the car... (Head in the car) After wiping my mouth and cleaning my man, I woke up and we were passing FireKeepers Casino near Marshall, MI. At this point I was unsure of where we were going. My first thought was maybe a room in the Chi or an event. I realized that he did pay for me to get my nails done two days ago, made us get up early for breakfast, and that convo, so I knew something good was bound to happen.

As we got closer to the downtown Battle Creek, MI exit, as I'm inhaling the smell of cereal, he asked for my mom's address. She moved back there about a year ago and I hadn't seen her since, so I immediately thought he surprised me with a visit. I told him 123 Ann St. Eight minutes later we were pulling up to her driveway and there were like seven to eight other cars there. Jakari said, "I told your mom to tell everybody we were coming. I figured that we both had the weekend off and you haven't seen your friends and family in a while. We see my parents once a month so here we are my baby. I hope you aren't upset."

"Of course not! I am so happy to have such a thoughtful man in my life." I kissed him and got out the car. At this point, Jakari pulled the camera back out.

My mom ran out the house and almost tackled me. Then came Michele, Foxy, my brother and sisters, and cousins.

I'm like man, he did this all on his own. It took all of my emotional strength to hold back my tears. I went into the house for a minute to see how my mother was living, but then somebody was calling my name to come outside. As I headed out, I can see out the window that the radio station van was outside, cameras were set and flashing and "You Are" by Charlie Wilson was playing softly in the background out of somebody's car.

     In the middle of the yard Jakari stood with his right arm fully extended in my direction. I walked towards him as the tears ran down my face. When I reached him, he grabbed my left hand and slowly took a bow to one knee. I remember it almost verbatim, he said, "You are a beautiful, funny, sexy, and intelligent woman. By far our good days outweigh our bad ones. I couldn't imagine another man loving you like I do. We go good together and we'll grow even better together. I want to grow old with you and share the rest of our lives together. Dasia Lanae Lovelace, will you do me the honor of being my wife? WILL YOU MARRY ME BABE?"

He was squeezing my hand so tight that my fingers looked all wrinkled. But of course I said, "YES!" He put this beautiful large stone on my finger and I was in awe, the crowd cheered, balloons were in the air, and cameras were flashing.

He kissed me and whispered, "It's you and me babe, until the end." I felt a tear run down his cheek and we just hugged for so long, as if no one else was there.

Chapter 8 - This is MY MAN!!!

Wow, being engaged was like already being married. This man treated me so good from the time I opened my eyes in the morning until we laid our heads to rest at night. I was blessed. I had a great man, a great career, and God was continuing to bless, but you know the Devil has to try and steal your joy every chance he gets and the keyword was try.

A few months after getting engaged Dave got out of being incarcerated and was very persistent about trying to rekindle the flames. He fully knew my relationship minus the fact that I was engaged to be married. At first I paid him no attention after countless numbers of emails, texts, and phone calls, but then I suddenly felt like something was missing and considered that something to be him. I admit I was curious to see him, hug him, etc. See this is where most women or people mess up at because they are so determined to rebuild their past, they won't accept the present and build for a better future. Crazy huh?

The devil was stirring up a recipe for disaster on my home front but he would not get me too easily. Six months after being engaged, my fiancé had to move to Los Angeles, CA as a part of job training and he would be there for 20 weeks. Sheeessh... I couldn't leave with him because I had to work at the station and continue to build my career. Working was a strong part of my livelihood and I had made a name for myself in the city of Detroit, so I couldn't just up and leave. So that we didn't lose our viewers, we both filmed from different locations and also included some of our face timing moments.

Dave tried and tried while my bae was gone, and I finally gave in. I allowed him to take me to lunch, which was a horrible decision because it eventually led to more than I was expecting. During lunch he stated how much he missed me and loved me. I told him I would always love him but that I wasn't in love with him and that my heart was already taken. *shaking my head*. He wasn't trying to hear any of that. He said that if he had never gotten locked up it would be us getting married and that if I gave him some time, it could still be us. It was all too much for me over lunch, so I stood up and said I was leaving.

He immediately stood up and as I passed his seat, he grabbed me swiftly, pulled me close to him and kissed me so good to the point that it scared me. Literally I was scared, because he turned me on so quickly. I'm talking, like I was instantly wet, and my heart was pumping fast, but my emotions were not all of pleasure. It was also confusion. I couldn't understand how another man could turn me on? I am human though.

All this bs went through my mind in like four seconds flat. I snapped out of my daze, speed walked to the car, and turned on, "Devil Get Up Off Me" as I burnt rubber out of the parking lot.

When I spoke with my Hunny that night I felt the urge to tell him what happened. However, I said nothing. Especially after I read some of D's text messages, inviting me on trips and various outings. Basically, begging for some of my time and swearing he could not care less about having sex with me, but I could already see the darkness at the end of the tunnel.

I couldn't help but think that spending time with him would be like going through some emotional trenches. Before I ended the call with my babe, I told him I loved him so much and that I couldn't wait to see him and his sexy dick. Out of the blue he was like, "What do you have on?"

My eyebrows raised and I said, "One of your t-shirts and some panties."

"I'm horny, can you help me?" I literally laughed out loud and then asked, "What do you want me to do babe?"

He then snickered. Before I knew it, my fingers were surfboarding in my wishing pool and he was grunting hard. Seven minutes later he moaned, "I'm about to cum,"

And I moaned, "I love you." as I drenched two of my fingers and the bed sheets. Gasping for air, I immediately laughed.

"What is so funny?"

I said, "Sometimes you have to laugh to keep from crying. I love everything about you.

It's the little things you do that keeps me so deeply in love with you and you don't even know it."

"So you liked that huh," he said?

"Of course I did…you probably thought I wouldn't do it."

"Yeah," he said, "But I'm so glad you did. Thank you. Now wipe my juices off and sleep tight. Good night my baby." I said good night, followed his instructions and went straight to bed.

I slept like a baby that night. The next morning, I woke up to several text messages and three voicemails. Dave was trippin' hard. The message that caught my attention said something like, "I bet you were on the phone with THAT NIGGA all night *shaking my head*

Oh, I hopped on the phone so quickly to chew his ass out. I'm talking before I even showered, brushed my teeth, or anything. I WAS HEATED. THEN BOOM!!! IT HIT ME AGAIN. I KNEW I WAS IN LOVE!!! Because I was ready to cuss a NIGGA out for disrespecting MY MAN. Speaking of him as if he was a nobody, PLEASE. Dave could have several seats with that bs.

I called and told him don't ever fuckin' speak of my man like that and that he was out of line. I also added that he's not a nigga. He is my dude, my guy, my love, my fiancé, and let's keep it all the way hood, that's my muthafuckin man! He acted as if I was blowing things out of proportion, but I just asked that he leave me alone. I didn't

108

want to have any problems with him, I just wanted him to know that I was happy where I was and that our time together had passed. It was great, or overall it was ok considering his incarceration, but I was engaged to be married and needed to focus on my future with my future husband.

I told him I hoped we never have to have a conversation like this again. He laughed, but I was pissed for real. During the call I barely let him get a word in but I caught a few statements of his like, "f him and f you"…lol…I let those things slide because people say a lot of things out of frustration so it didn't bother me much. However, he apologized and I accepted but then disconnected and blocked his number. Maybe that was the sign I needed to reassure me that I was making the right decision and that my life was headed down the right path. I prayed that God continued to bless me and my relationship. I also prayed that he brought Jakari and me closer to him.

***

The engagement process was still going smoothly, we shared a social media account, shared a home, and countless lovable memories. So now the wedding was less than four months away, I get on Facebook (what a horrible idea) and come across a meme that stated, "Do you still keep in contact with your first?" Out of curiosity I searched Shawn Feltner and a picture popped up. My dumbass just had to go a little further, so I inboxed him a message like, "Ayyyyeeee" to see if he remembered me. Honestly, I felt like our time may not have been as memorable to him. But au contraire mon frère.

His response was, "Wooooowwww Dasia DL Lovelace. I'm speechless. I can't believe this is really you. I just looked through your pics quickly and you are beautiful. Damn so you are getting ready to get married? No disrespect but I would love to see you in person!"

No lie, I looked at his profile picture twice and said, "A quick visit wouldn't hurt." We exchanged numbers and I immediately deleted the thread. Swear to God he was still super sexy but I had no idea on what I was getting myself into!!

Three weeks later I get a text message stating, "Hey this is Shawn are you ready to see me yet?"

I replied, "Don't say it like that, but we can meet up sometime this week." He asked if I still like to shoot pool and I said yes, so he suggested to meet in the city at the

Magic Stick on Saturday. I insisted that we meet up on Thursday because I didn't want to be seen there on the weekend. Thursday came and I was super nervous and curious; and for some strange reason wanted to tell Jakari. I went anyways…When I pulled up, he was there to greet me at the door. I was stunned, he looked like a male model, with perfect teeth, beautiful eyes, and those same strong arms and chest. I shyly greeted him and we went inside. I ordered a drink or two and we played pool while chatting for about two hours.

During our last game he asked if I was happy in my relationship. I firmly said yes and he said well how do you know? I said just trust me, I know. He then came and pressed himself up against me as I was getting ready to shoot my shot and I quickly moved. He said, "What's wrong? You don't find me attractive anymore?"

I jokingly replied, "Can you move so I can shoot my shot, little ugly ass boy?" We both laughed. I knocked the eight ball in and told him that it was nice seeing him, but I needed to get home to my fiancé. He asked if he could see me again and I said probably not.

I hugged him gently, but he squeezed me tightly and whispered in my ear, "I want you." My eyes got big, I tried to push him away but he tightened his grip. He then whispered, "That curly haired, soft ass dude, can't fuck you like I can." I was shocked, appalled, and disappointed in myself for even meeting up with him.

"Watch your mouth and let me go so we don't make a scene." He let me go and I quickly left. An hour later he sent a text stating that I meet him at The Renaissance, room number 711 at midnight tomorrow or he is posting a pic of me that he took while we were shooting pool and telling my husband that we fucked. I responded simply asking why he would lie and do that? His response, I was acting like I'm too good to give him the pussy and he didn't like my attitude earlier.

I'm thinking, what kind of petty crap is this guy on?? I was super stressed. All I kept thinking was should I tell my homegirls, should I tell Jakari, should I call my brother… I didn't know what to do and I felt like I was helpless; but I knew for sure that I wasn't giving him anything. He was the devil in a fine man's body!! One thing's for sure and two things for certain, that I love Jakari and I wasn't going to let this ruin our plans for the future. The next morning, I decided that I was going to tell babe what happened, show him the blackmailing text, and if he broke up with me then I was going to that room alone. If he stood by my side, then WE were going to the room. To make a long story short, around 11:30pm that night Jakari came out the bedroom with a .45 on his hip (that I didn't know he had), grabbed his jacket, and said get your coat and let's go!!

All hell broke loose at the damn hotel. The car ride home was completely silent. Jakari turned the music off, rolled his window down, and kept looking at me and smacking his lips. As soon as we got home and through the doors, he went in on me HARD! "So that's what you like huh? Thug ass niggas huh? Well I'm sorry, I'm not a thug ass nigga!" he said in a very angry and disappointed tone. I am a grown ass man, and it's a strong possibility I just threw my life

115

away trying to protect or defend your silly ass! Why were you even out with this guy? I didn't respond so he screamed, ANSWER THE FUCKIN QUESTION DASIA!! I was just crying and dumbfounded and couldn't find the right words to say.

Jakari was standing in the bathroom looking at his wounds and I was in the bedroom, but next thing you know he was right in my face with his eyes fire red and a small stream of blood running down the side of his forehead yelling, "ANSWER THE GOD DAMN QUESTION!"

"I don't know, in my mind it seemed harmless and I am so sorry babe".

"Did you ever consider how this would look if one of our viewers/fans seen us, if one of my friends or your coworkers' seen us?" I shook my head no. At this point I was disgusted with myself for so many reasons. My heart belonged to Jakari and I couldn't even fathom the thought of loving another man. Jakari is intelligent, sexy, freaky, employed, and FAITHFUL. Most important he loves me unconditionally, but I can tell that things would be different.

The thought that Jakari might catch a case over me made me sick to my stomach. To be clear, I'm still placing a good portion of the blame on Shawn. Once we got to the room, I knocked on the door, and when he opened and noticed that Jakari was with me, he tried to shut it quickly but we pushed right through. Jakari immediately stated, "I saw your messages, and I know you didn't fuck my woman. Leave us alone, go back to whatever you were doing in life before yesterday and we won't have any problems".

"Or what? Shawn said.

"Or you and I are going to have some problems bro".

Shawn laughed and said, "Yeah alright, you can take your bitch and leave now"

Within a blink of eye Jakari had smacked the shit of Shawn across his face and followed it with a punch that landed right under his eye. Shawn stumbled a bit and took Jakari down as he was falling to the ground. They began to tussle around on the floor and Shawn did get some hits in, but eventually Jakari pulled out his gun and hit him over the head twice. I helped Jakari up and we left Shawn laying there bleeding from the head, but he was still moving. As we were leaving out of the hotel, I told the front desk that I heard a lot of commotion, and I think that the man in room 711 needs help quickly.

I cried myself to sleep for so many nights. About two weeks later, I sent Michele and Foxy both long emails about the situation and I told them that Jakari and I are ok. In the email I also stated that Shawn is still alive (I knew because he posted pictures on Facebook), the police never contacted us and that we would eventually talk about it, but I wasn't sure when. They both begged to come by and blew up my phone for a week straight, but I didn't answer. I was so angry with myself. I couldn't just let the past be the past. Normally the shoe is on the other foot and the man is in this predicament but not this time because my dumbass had to be different.

Two stressful months had gone by and I was starting to fear that Jakari was going to leave me or might already be sleeping around with someone else. He damn sure hadn't touched me during the two months and he has been sleeping on the couch or in the guest bedroom. Lately he has been staying out longer and spending money frivolously as if it's not October and the wedding is scheduled for December 31st, 2018. He has purchased a new expensive watch, that I noticed while we happen to be in the kitchen at the same time. He even got diamonds put into his Cartier frames and took a trip to Chicago (unrelated to work) for a few days.

Foxy kept texting, asking if the wedding was still on but I didn't respond because I didn't know. Jakari had completely shut me out of his life. When blogging, he would turn the camera towards me for a few seconds, basically to show the world that I was still alive and that we are still under one roof. I would hear him make comments about how we are going through some things right now or how some women don't appreciate a good man. Honestly, I have tried everything to get back on his good side. Instead of telling you detail by detail, I'll just give you a list:

1. I purchased him an outfit and tickets to the Sada Baby concert. One for him and one for a friend.
2. I tried wearing lingerie and dancing for him, but he politely asked that I stop and go to my room.
3. I wrote him a letter of apology.
4. I called his mom and my mom but they both said just give him some time.
5. I got him a new camera and a carrying case.

Nothing was working and I was tired of it!

The week before Halloween my boss asked what was Jakari and I wearing to the annual costume party and I told him I wasn't sure but just know that we will be fresh to DEATH. When I got home, Jakari was sitting on the couch and I used the party topic to break the ice. To my surprise, he said we can go, and from there I began to cry. I told him I was so sorry and begged him to still marry me. I could feel the mascara trickling down my face and I could taste the salty tears. I desperately wanted him to know right then and there that I understand that I hurt him and put us in a horrible situation but I promise to never do it again if he just lets me back in his life! I was literally on my knees!

Jakari grabbed my hand and said stand up. He walked me into the guest bathroom grabbed a towel and began to wipe my face, but the tears kept coming. Then he finally let go and told me how he truly felt without screaming and cussing at me. He said, "I miss you babe and I know it's taken me a while to say this, but I forgive you. At first I couldn't figure out why you had even gone to see him, but then I eventually thought that if it was me, I probably would've gone too. And I also kept thinking that he didn't sleep with you, but a part of me was thinking what type of vibes were you giving off to even make him think that he could."

I interrupted stating, "Nothing, he only pushed up on me once while shooting pool and I quickly shut him down. I swear I would've never seen this coming from him, but I pray that you believe me when I say that I am all yours for the rest of my life."

Jakari kept whispering I'm sorry while slowly lifting up my skirt and kissing

123

my neck. I was waaay past due, so it only took seconds for me nipples to turn into Hershey Kisses, while my lower half was turning into a love pool. He backed me up against the sink and made love so good. You could hear the juices with every stroke and I always seem to get wetter every time Jakari moaned in my ear. This time I heard him say, this is your dick and yours only. I did realize that he didn't have on a condom, but I trusted him to be smart enough to pull out! To my surprise, he came in me and grunted so hard! I was shocked, satisfied, and in disbelief all at the same. Another tear fell down my face as he stood there holding me, but not because of the sex but because I looked to my left and there was a used rubber in the trash can!!

OMG it felt like a blow to the chest. I was breathing so hard and the tears were still flowing. "Are you ok?" he asked.

"I'm good babe, thank you."

"Are you sure?"

"I need a drink!!"

Jakari removed all of his clothing, walked over to the shower and turned the water on. He turned around and waved me over. So, I took off my clothes and got into the shower with him. As soon as we got in, he was right back hard and ready for action. I was thinking did he pop a pill or something? He turned the shower head down some and actually sat down in the shower and motioned for me to sit on his face. Of course, I did, but in the back of my mind I was thinking did someone else do this to him, in our shower?

We had never done that exact position in the shower before. My mind was all over the place. After I came, he stood up, and picked me up simultaneously. Jakari walked us both into the water and fucked me like he was auditioning for a porno movie. The tears fell again and for the second time, he came in me without a rubber. Therefore, it was clear to me that he was trying to get me pregnant and I wasn't sure how I felt about that seeing as though the rubber in the trash can indicates that he fucked someone else, in our home!!

We both stood silently breathing for about five minutes. I had so many mixed emotions. Eventually, I washed, got out the shower, blow dried my hair, put it in two ponytails and went to the kitchen to fix a drink! After all that had taken place, I needed a strong drink! Honestly, I felt sick to my stomach. All I kept thinking is that I'd never sleep with another man. I didn't even want to. But I also thought that it was all my fault. Had I never gone to meet Shawn, everything would still be perfect, but we can't change the past. A part of me was thinking to just

pack my stuff and leave, but my body
wouldn't allow me to move.

I was glued to the couch with a glass
of Hennessey for three hours straight. Off
and on, my legs were going numb and it felt
like I couldn't breathe. I swear to God I was
having real life panic attacks! Broken
hearted, I was. I've heard so many stories
about people being cheated on but had
personally never experienced the pain. Not in
a hundred years would I have wished that
pain on someone because there is no
medicine, drink, or kind words that can heal a
broken heart. It took everything out of me to
not scream, cry hard, and cuss him out. Jakari
asked me if I was ok multiple times and I
said yes, and that I wanted to be alone. The
thought of some other woman rubbing her
fingers through his hair, kissing him, licking

C.T.

his neck, sucking him up, and taking his dick was so surreal.

Chapter 9 – I Can Get Passed This

I got a text from a co-worker asking what we were wearing to the party and that's what broke my state of depression. I replied you'll see and went into the bedroom to discuss it with Jakari. I told him we should be Sanaa Lathan and Omar Epps from the movie Love & Basketball. He agreed with no dispute, so I went online and ordered a white USC crewneck sweater with the maroon letters. Of course I already owned some jeans and Jakari has a black Nike sweat suit and a grey tee. Really, all we needed was a basketball for our photos, so I asked Jakari to pick up one before Halloween. He said ok and we didn't say another word to each other for the rest of the night.

C.T.

The next day I woke up feeling a little better. I asked Jakari if all of his people had been fitted for their suits and if everything was good on his end.

He said, "Everything is paid for and that all you need to do is show up."

"Is that right?" I said with kind of an attitude.

"Come here."

I walked over, "What's up, you know I'm trying to get ready for work."

"What's wrong sweetheart, did I do something wrong?"

Instead of saying what was on my heart, "No and sorry for being so snippy." I then told him that everything was good on my end as well. Michele, Foxy and my cousin Fiya had all been fitted for their dresses and the DJ, planner, photographer, etc had all been booked. So now I am just anticipating the bachelorette party! I could tell he was relieved to hear that everything was still going as planned…

Well a few days had gone by and it was time for the costume party. I'm really not too fond of partying on a weekday but oh well. We went live almost the entire time at the party. Since we started vlogging our viewers have gone from a few thousand to now having a few hundred thousand subscribers to our channel, whom we share a good majority of our life with. A lot of people were so happy to see us together and there were a few haters and trolls, but it comes with the territory. I did have a good time at the party with Jakari and our Love & Basketball costumes won us 3rd place, which got us a $500 Visa card. Truthfully, even with all the fun and excitement, I still kept having thoughts of him playing me. I still wanted to confront him, slap him, cuss him out, and then tell him I love him. I digress.

Anyways, from that night forward things were decent until a month before the wedding. I then received threatening text messages from Shawn stating that Karma is a bitch, he doesn't forgive me and that its over for Jakari. More so, he kept implying that he would do something to us and claimed that he would crash our wedding. I urged him to leave us alone and told him that all of this was uncalled for and that he should let it go. He didn't respond, so I just prayed to God he would leave us the hell alone. Some dudes can be so petty and annoying for no legitimate reason.

Forget Shawn, things were going great. I told nobody about the text. I just blocked his number and focused on my big day, but I'm talking about the bachelorette party right now, not the wedding. I'm not sure what they had planned but I do know that some shirts arrived from DBW's printing in Battle Creek, so I knew my mom was involved. The package came with four black tees. One read BRIDE with gold glitter and the other three read BRIDESMAID in red glitter. In my opinion, they were absolutely beautiful, and I sent a text to Foxy telling her that I was too geeked about the shirts. I called my mom to try and fish for some information, but she didn't give in. She simply stated to have fun but not too much fun because we needed to be in somebody's church on the next morning. Please believe that I was going to tell everyone that she said that so we could have a good laugh. My mom knew good and well that we were going to be too lit!!

A few more days had gone by and Jakari and I were still getting along just fine. However, there were days when my insecurities would get the best of me. Like days, when he was working late, or when I was working, and he was home alone. Since the rubber incident, he has given me no reason to think that he was cheating but I had no reason to think that prior either. My mind was still all over the place but there was no doubt in my mind that I was going to marry him! Daily I was just doing my best to look towards a beautiful future.

The Thursday before the bachelorette weekend (not party, because they had a whole weekend planned) started off great!

That morning I woke up to the satin sheets hugging my naked body so perfectly and feeling oh so good. Since I sleep with the window cracked a little, the cold air had my nipples standing at attention. Now I know it may sound odd, but I hate morning breath, so I got up brushed my teeth and got right back in bed for a little more rest. I was almost into a deep sleep when I felt his soft tongue flick across my clit, and I flinched.

The second time I opened my legs a little more but kept my eyes closed and he kept licking while I moaned in ecstasy. The way he palms my titties just does something to me. I yelled out "Alexa play my slow jam playlist" and the first song to play was "All the time" by Jeremih and Lil Wayne. Once the song began to play, Jakari stopped with the feasting and without hesitation began to make love to me. It felt so magical, I know it sounds weird or childish to say but I'm serious. It felt perfect, and I squirted something juicy! That doesn't happen all the time but when it does... Ouuuu shhhhh, it was all on his stomach and the bed.

Oh and I probably never mentioned it but my baby can dance too (like a stripper). As he rolled his hips and slow stroked, I couldn't do anything but hold him closely and enjoy. Next thing you know he stopped again and walked us over to the chair, he sat down and then I sat down right on top of it. By this time Keith Sweat's, Nobody, was playing and he whispered in my ear show your future husband what you can do. So I stood up off him a little but not off it and began to slowly bounce on it while grabbing my own titties while he licked all over them. He whispered what else, so I turned around and put my hands on his knees and started throwing it back. Oh that had him moaning so good, he pulled me back towards him and started kissing me but now he was doing all the work.

I can tell he was ready to cum, because he always asks first, so he said, "Do you want me to cum?"

I whispered, "Yes."

"Where?" (which is a question he's never asked before).

"Anywhere you want," I said. He pulled it out quickly and began to shoot it on my titties, but before he could finish, I had all of him in my mouth and was sucking up every drop. He moaned OH SHIT so loud and pulled my hair so tight, that I know he was loving it and that it took him by surprise. Jakari slapped me on my ass so hard that I

137

knew he left a print. He tried to kiss me, but I wouldn't let him because first I needed to go spit and gargle. For some reason, I just couldn't swallow but when I tell you that it was by far one of our best performances yet, I am not lying.

We took a shower, changed the sheets on the bed and laid there for another hour and a half or so. When I woke up Jakari was already dressed and heading out the door. He kissed me goodbye and said, "Just remember you have your own private dancer and porn star at home; just in case you get any crazy thoughts while out at your bachelorette activities."

As he was walking to the door, I yelled, "Is that why you put me to sleep like that?"

He just chuckled, said I love you, and went out the door. I smiled, got up, and realized that he already had my outfit hanging up on the bathroom door. Jakari had out my favorite black and white striped pencil skirt and red blouse. He seems to always make me feel some type of way when he dresses me, it's unexplainable. This man even had out his favorite black pumps of mine. My smile stretched from ear to ear. I started to call and ask why but I figured that I didn't want to spoil the vibe that we had going so I just got dressed and headed to work.

To my surprise they had my office covered with decorations and everyone was there. My coworkers had set up a wedding party of their own. There were balloons, gifts, a cake, and my man. Jakari was there wearing a pair of black jeans, a white dress shirt, and a red tie to compliment the outfit that he left out for me. I found myself constantly taking deep breaths because I was so in awe. We shared a few minutes of the party with our viewers. It was really beautiful. I thanked everyone for their gifts. My boss also told me that I had the rest of the week off so I was super geeked. Everyone kept telling Jakari how much I brag about him and that I'm a good woman, etc. I really felt blessed.

Truthfully, because of that one incident, I wasn't sure he believed that I was still a good woman. Despite the good love making, unprotected sex, and the party, I was still concerned. Let's be honest, as humans, we can forgive but not forget. I still hadn't said anything to anyone about the condom, so daily I was walking around with this in the back of mind... Anyways, thanks to my boss, my weekend was starting early and I was so in need of the next few days with my girls.

Once we left the office, Jakari took me out to lunch. We spent at least two hours inside this hibachi restaurant over in Novi. He talked about how he was so happy to have me in his life and that he only wants to be with me. He also stated, "We BOTH have made mistakes," but he wants to grow old with me. My first thought was to question his mistakes, but again I said nothing. By the time he finished his second long island, he was sitting right next to me vs sitting across from me! Jakari was throwing out random compliments, like, "Have I ever told you that I get lost in your beautiful brown eyes," or "Every time you lick your lips, I just want to lick them too because they are so damn sexy," or "The way you speak is so intriguing because it's the perfect combination between

141

sophistication, a hint of ghetto, and a splash of freakiness."

"I love everything about you and all I can say is I love you too and I love the thought of spending the rest of my life with you." Jakari extended his hand to me as if he wanted me to get up so I gave him the strange look of curiosity, you know the one where one eyebrow is raised. I wiped my mouth and stood up, he grabbed his phone and put on "A Couple of Forevers" by Chrisette Michele and we danced right there in the middle of the day, in the middle of the restaurant as if we were the only ones there.

We rocked to a little two step together until the song ended and once we stopped the people were clapping and I was again in awe. We went back to our seats, had the waitress bring the bill, paid, and left. In the car we held hands the entire way home. I was on cloud nine and felt like my day couldn't get any better... Until I walked into my house and found Fiya, Michelle, and Foxy all chillin' with glasses of wine in their hands. We all screamed with excitement and it was on from there. Don't worry, I am going to give you all a play by play of our weekend.

Thursday night we decided to hangout as a group. Jakari called some fellas and we ended up at Starters for drinks and food. I'm glad we all agreed on Starters because I absolutely love the steak bites there and the drinks are above average. There's really not much to tell, but Fiya did tell Jakari that she knew he was the one because he was all I talked about after meeting him. Michele and Foxy agreed but these ignoramuses also added that before Dave got locked, they thought he was the one too. All I kept saying

143

to myself was, "Lord make them stop talking before it gets awkward in here". Luckily, we finished the night on a good note. Everybody had a good time and it was priceless.

Chapter 10-It Was Time To Turn Up!

The next morning, we were up, dressed, and out the door. We all rode with Foxy because she had a truck, which of course had the most room. Honestly, I didn't know where we were going but I was packed for all different climates and events. The car ride allowed us to play catch up in each other's lives. Yeah, we talk on the phone but it's not the same as seeing someone's facial expressions and body language when they are telling you something. I'm not sure about everyone else but it was very therapeutic for me.

Well… we ended up in Chicago and it looked beautiful. The girls had booked a suite downtown and it was lavish. When we arrived at the room, there were balloons shaped like penises, candy penises on the table, four freshly made margaritas with straws shaped like penises. I couldn't stop laughing, especially when Fiya busted out her lie stating that she didn't start sucking dick until I told her about how wet it makes me get ...smh I almost spit my drink out while laughing and yelling, "That bitch is lying!"

That night we ended up at this night club where we heard some slam poetry (which was the bomb) and a few comedians that had me cracking up. We left the club and headed to the Cheesecake Factory for a late dinner and drinks. Anytime I'm at that restaurant I have to order my favorite, but before I could, the waiter was placing four lemon drops on our table. My girls know me oh too well. While eating Michele noticed that a guy kept looking my way, so she got up and invited him over. The first thing he said was, "You are very beautiful and so is that ring, is your man here tonight"?

I replied, "I don't know what you all are trying to do but I'm not going for it."

He said, "For what?"

"For this. I do not plan on doing any cheating tonight, so thanks but no thanks."

This fool said, "What about tomorrow?" I laughed and said please leave.

All three of them were laughing and giggling like high school girls. Foxy says, "Dang so Jakari is hitting it like that?" I gave her a stern YES and demanded that they finish their drinks, we were still on round one and they were on bs already.

Michele then says, "You've never had a one-night stand right?"

I chuckled no and I'm not interested. Fiya says, "Ok don't try to call me three years from now crying saying that you cheated on Jakari and had a one-night stand with a sexy stallion."

I damn near choked on my drink again and said, "Listen here, I will not be cheating on my bachelorette getaway and if I do ever decide to cheat, I promise to take it to my grave and not tell a soul!" I ended my statement by demonstrating the mic drop with my hands so that they got the picture. I told ya'll before that we were a mess together. After dinner we headed back to the hotel and I stayed up for probably about a half hour talking to my babe and telling him about my night. He was at the house watching Sports Center because his big day wasn't until Saturday. I don't remember much about the conversation because I think I fell asleep on him.

I woke up the next morning with Foxy asking for everybody to hurry up and shower but only put on your panties and bras, and come out with your robes. Fiya, said "Oh hell no, I'm not rubbing or painting anybody else's feet." We all laughed. I was curious to see what else these women had planned. I must admit that they had been impressing me the entire trip. An hour later and we were all showered an in our robes. We sat down for breakfast, which was delivered by room service and 30 minutes later we get a knock on the door and eight beautiful men came in. One Hershey chocolate, one banana pudding, two white chocolates, and four smooth peanut butter pecan cuties. Jesus, these men were gorgeous. They set up four individual stations, with massage tables, and room dividers so that we couldn't see each other, but we could still hear and converse if we wanted. There were two guys for each woman, and they let me pick my two!

So I picked one of the white chocolates and the delicious looking Hershey man. We were instructed to disrobe and lay on our stomachs, and each person was given a stop word that could be used if something was being done to you that you didn't want to happen. From there it was pleasure in paradise. I was given the word big daddy, clever right, that they would make you say "big daddy out loud, but it's meant for them to stop.

White chocolate massaged my back and neck, while Mr. Hershey massaged from my ass down. One of the peanut butter pecan cuties that was massaging Foxy announced loudly that we have prepared three strong mimosas for each woman so just raise your hand if you want one and we'll make it happen. I immediately raised my hand. The massage was feeling awesome. Michele yelled, "Give the bride to be the extra treatment, put your finger in her ass or something and don't worry Dasia, everybody washed their hands and used hand sanitizer."

Everybody laughed, but I whispered, "Please don't." They kept massaging and it was wonderful. We didn't really talk to each other but probably because it was feeling so good. The massage was much needed for me. Work and Jakari's sex game had me a little tense. White Chocolate kept saying "relax". I told him I was trying, so I took a deep breath, tried to loosen up, exhaled and asked if it was better? He said no and tickled me. I began to giggle and wiggle, and could hear Mr.

C.T.

Hershey Chocolate down there snickering, so I told him to hush up back there and keep rubbing my little booty. Quickly they both said, "It's not little," and then White Chocolate squeezed a little on my right cheek while the other guy squeezed the right and said, "Let's have some fun." White Chocolate swiftly unsnapped my bra and asked me to lift up a little bit. He removed my bra and threw it up and over to the left.

It ended up with Fiya and she said, "Aww shit." I mumbled OMG, just live in the moment Dasia. He then raised the table a couple of inches and while standing right in front of me he began to massage my breast. Instantly I began to fantasize about sucking him while the other guy ate me from the back. I had never had those thoughts before, but I had never had two sexy men massage my body while I was pretty much naked either!! I asked for another drink and Mr. Hershey handed one to me before I could blink an eye and then he asked, "What were you thinking about, what's on your mind?" I said nothing.

"So you have no thoughts about my boy standing in front of you like that?" I shook my head no (even though the print through his shorts really looked like the eggplant emoji. smh) "So you are not aroused at all huh?"

"Is that your goal," I asked?

"Yes, at your home girl's request." I told them I wasn't giving up nothing... "Oh we can accomplish our goal without penetration. Next thing you know White Chocolate was under the table sucking my titties while the dark skin guy rubbed my ass in such a seductive way that the juices began to flow and I couldn't control it. Mr. Hershey rubbed his thumb across my clit and I held my breath because I didn't want to be moaning in a room full of other people. To make a longer story short, it was like having a threesome without actually getting some! But I did let my guard down and they did manage to make me cum so hard that I left a puddle on the table. I was sooo freaking exhausted, relaxed, surprised, excited, impressed, and unremorseful. Right after I came, I watched Mr. Hershey Chocolate lick my juices off of his finger tips and the other licked his lips as one guy yelled, "It's a wrap ladies."

As quickly as they came was as quickly as they cleaned up and left. Before they left, White Chocolate whispered in my ear that I was super beautiful and left his phone number. Once they left, we took turns

showering and all took a nap for a few hours.
No one really discussed their massages.
Although, I did mention that mine was
unbelievable and that I thought White
Chocolate was the sexiest thing in the room
besides myself... I woke up rejuvenated and
realized that I had only exchanged a good
morning text with Jakari, so I dialed his
number. The phone rang once, and I hung up
but immediately hit the FaceTime button. He
popped up on the screen looking like a tall
glass of the finest cognac. We talked for a
few minutes and then I let him go so that he
could get ready for his big night.

Soon as I put my phone down
Michele asked, "So ya'll ready to hit the
clubs tonight?" I quickly said no thanks and
everybody started laughing. Fiya then told
Michele to pay her $20, because apparently,
they betted on whether or not I was going to

the club. Luckily, they already had it planned for someone to come to our room and do the wine and canvas thing. It was only 5pm and the painter wasn't coming until 7 so we ordered room service and decided to play catch up on each other's lives.

Actually, it went from playing catching up to, "So are you sure Jakari is the one? Has he ever hit you? Any side bitches? Is Shawn still stalking you and what really happened that night? Is the sex still the same? Do you have any doubts? Have you all discussed children? Have you all spoken with a counselor?"

I guess my guard was down the entire day because I told them everything and all I asked in return was for them to still love US the same and respect my decision. I told them that yes I love him and yes I want to spend the rest of my life with him. I let the nosey rosies know that Shawn doesn't stalk me, but he did make a threat to crash the wedding and I told them about that night. Lastly, I told them that Jakari had never physically hurt me, but I was sick when I found a condom in the trash! I felt sick to my stomach and my mental health was damaged for a while. Foxy began to state how her man cheated once and never stopped. I interrupted her and stated that all men are not the same and you don't have to stay! She said and neither do you, and I said you are so right and that's why I'm not leaving but you on the other hand are complaining as if you are unhappy. She said so are you! No, I am answering a question, but do you boo. The room fell silent for a little bit, and then Fiya eased the tension by saying just keep White Chocolate on stand by and you'll be good sis. I damn near choked on my drink laughing at her silly self.

The painter finally came, and he was sexy too. He kind of reminded you of Idris Elba. He was tall, dark, salt and pepper beard, with a physique of a fitness instructor. We painted a beautiful picture of a man on one knee in front of a woman. The top of her head wasn't in the picture, so you could only see her from the waist down. The instructor's picture had the woman in a red dress, her skin was like an off-white color, and she had A-cups. The guy in the pic had on black pants, black shirt, red bowtie and a red belt. Each of us painted ours a different color to have some individuality. My girl had on a blue dress, and the guy had on black pants and a blue shirt. I also put a tear stream down the side of his face because mine had to stand out more. All of our paintings were absolutely beautiful! Once the painting was over, Fiya and Foxy went out and Michele and I just sat around the room. I uploaded a video to our page and went to sleep. By the time I woke up it was 9:30 AM the next morning and to my surprise, everybody was up except for me.

After getting dressed, we headed out to this chicken and waffle restaurant that was delicious. The syrup had a nice, sweet, buttery, warm taste and the chicken was seasoned the way I like it. I took a picture of the menu, sent it to Jakari and said, "We have to come here". He replied, it looks fire. After breakfast we did a little shopping downtown. I think the best part was riding the U-Horse which is a horse and carriage version of Uber. It was TOO MUCH fun. Would you believe that they had almost every part of our trip planned out? I love these chicks.

C.T.

Oh, and I forget to mention we had our shirts on!! To be honest, even after going to all of those high-end clothing stores, my favorite gifts ended up coming from a boutique that had some MGHH Apparel. I got myself a black tee that read **Michigan Girl Hustle Harder** and Jakari a matching black tee that read **Michigan Guys Hustle Harder**. The way that the words were printed on the shirts reminded me of the logo for the show Martin, which is a classic in my eyes.

We returned from shopping, packed our bags, and were headed back to the city. I thought the trip was over until Michele said get off on this exit. Me and Fiya looked at each other with raised eyebrows. To make a long story short, we ended up stopping at The Little Ceasars Arena for a concert with Tank, Trey Songz, R. Kelly, Chris Brown, and August Alsina. I was sooo happy I cried. We even had backstage passes and I was all on Trey. Between me and you, August looked like he wanted me, for real for real. The entire weekend was unforgettable, the pictures, and memories are priceless. I just pray they know how appreciative I am!!

Once we reached my house, we all hugged and cried in the driveway. I told them to stop because I'll see them next week. I got inside and Jakari was watching Sports Center in my favorite grey boxer briefs, so you know what happened next. As soon as I laid my bags down, he laid me down!

Chapter 11- The Big Day!

It feels so good to be in love… a week had gone by so quickly and the day was here. My family was in town and so was his. I was so nervous that my hands and armpits were sweating profusely. Everybody kept telling me to relax but for some reason I couldn't. My Uncle Shawn called and said are you sure you want to go through with this. I laughed and said yes. He said, "Hey I asked him the same question when Jakari talked to me about proposing." I laughed even harder.

I said, "You just make sure you get here to walk me down the aisle." This man said I called to make sure I don't waste my gas coming there and you done changed your mind. He definitely eased the mood for me some with his corny jokes.

It wasn't that I was having second thoughts or anything, it was that I barely had any time to think to myself. People's flights were delayed, others were running late, Jakari texted that he took a shot or two to relax, and the wedding planner was asking me a thousand questions. Finally, I created a voicemail that gave Michele and Fiya's number for questions and concerns. I also advised the wedding planner to direct all of her questions to them as well.

We arrived at the church about 9:00 AM. The ceremony was held at the Church of God in Christ off East Main St. near St. Claire Shores. The sun was shining bright and it was as cold as I was expecting. I made sure that my mom brought Amari G from

Battle Creek with her to do my hair and makeup. As I walked through the aisles, it was all perfect. The flowers on the side of the pews were a pure snow-white color (I don't recall the type of flower), and they looked flawless. I had no complaints at all. There are things that I could have complained about, but it wasn't worth my time. The wedding was set to start at 11:00AM and we were running on schedule, the pastor was there, my bridesmaids, were there and so were all the groomsmen.

Everybody else were spectators. I put on my dress and I was absolutely amazed. The dress was an ivory color with Chantilly lace sleeves, a V-neck cut in the front and back, with a 5-foot detachable train. I made sure it fit just right so that I wasn't stiff all day in the dress because that would irritate me. My hair was pinned up in a cute bun, and

I had on a pair of pearl earrings that were given to me from grandmother before she passed.

I heard three hard knocks on the door like it was the police, so I knew it was my Uncle Shawn. Before anybody could yell, "WHO IS IT?" he said, "I'm just letting you know that I'm ready and waiting for you." My mom gathered Amari and me, and said a prayer before I left the room. I opened the door and told him that I was ready. Since I knew the tears would be falling, I put a Kleenex in my right hand. Seeing others cry, always makes me cry too. We headed towards the sanctuary and I could hear everyone as they rose to attention, and the photographer was snapping pictures the whole way down the hall. The doors opened, I took a huge deep breath, and I began to walk down the aisle as the speakers played,

C.T.

"This Is Why I Love You", by Major. Cameras were flashing and I could barely get a look at the nearly 300 people that were in attendance, but it didn't matter because Jakari had all of my attention.

Usually people are always saying how good the bride looks but I was truly mesmerized by him. Jakari had on an Ivory colored jacket, a white shirt, black bowtie, and black pants. My man was clean! I am so lucky to have my physical attraction match my emotions! After 23 steps down the aisle, Uncle Shawn handed me off to Jakari. He took my hand and whispered in my ear, "You look stunning."

"Thank you babe, you look good too." The whole crowd went "aaawwweee" and it reminded us immediately that we had small microphones on because we were filming live for our viewers.

Jakari and I had written our own vows, so the pastor said a few words and asked that Jakari read his first. I remember it verbatim.

"Ms. Dasia, I want to spend the rest of my life with you. You are an extremely beautiful, kind, fun, loving, educated, sexy, God-fearing, forgiving woman. You are everything I could've ever imagined in a wife. You honestly make me so happy. Truthfully, I couldn't see myself living on this earth without you as my wife and that's why we are here today. If I have ever given you any doubt that you aren't the only woman for me, please forgive me. I will love you through sickness and health. And I will love you and only you until death tears us apart! I love you my beautiful queen...

And then it was my turn. I had already put in my special request to have Foxy fan me while I spoke, so my eyes could stay dry. It did help some.

Jakari, the love of my life. I love you in a way that I have never loved a man before. You love me and all my flaws. Honestly, shortly after I met you, I prayed that you were the one. I stopped and took a huge deep breath to control my emotions while Foxy fanned harder. Our good days, surely out-weighs our bad days and I have no complaints. I want to grow old with you and love you until there is no more breath in my body. You are a beautiful reflection of me, as I am to you. I don't know what I would do

without you and I never want to find out. I
want you forever.

The pastor whispered rings please.
Jakari's best man/cousin Eric handed him the
rings.

The pastor then said, "Jakari Leon
Taylor, do you take Dasia Lanae Lovelace to
be your wife?"

Jakari cleared his throat and said, "I
absolutely do," and I placed a ring on his
finger.

The pastor then turned to me and said,
"Dasia Lanae Lovelace do you take Jakari
Leon Taylor to be your husband?"

I said, "I DO!" Jakari must have
blinked 11 times before a tear crept down the
side of his face as he stood there squeezing
my hand so tightly. He stayed looking down

at his feet for what felt like five minutes but was more like 20 seconds. I released my hands from his and used my Kleenex to clear the tear. He chuckled and said, "You always have your man covered huh?"

"At all times," I responded, and my husband placed the most gorgeous diamond ring on my finger and then grabbed my hands so tightly.

"Does anyone object to the union of these two? Speak now or forever hold your peace." I heard a cough, and the whole sanctuary turned around. Shawn was there! He said nothing, but his presence was enough to rub me the wrong way. In the back of my mind, I felt like a sinner because this was supposed to be the best day of my life, but all I kept thinking was, "We should have killed his ass in the hotel room."

I could tell that it bothered Jakari by the way he kept clenching his teeth and giving me the death stare. I whispered, "Just focus on OUR day," and we continued. The pastor stated, by the powers vested in me I now pronounce you as husband and wife, you may now kiss your bride young man." Jakari pulled me in closer and placed a kiss on my lips that will be unforgettable until the end of time. We turned around to face our loved ones and the Pastor, pretty much shouted, Mr. and Mrs. Taylor as we preceded to leave the sanctuary.

While leaving the church, I immediately looked to my right, and there Shawn was with a smirk on his face. I paid him no attention, I was looking good, feeling good, and there was no way I was going to let him steal my happiness. Jakari and I stayed back to take a few pictures outside of the

church, as the limo waited for us. Luckily,
we only had to drive a short distance to the
venue where our reception was being held.
On our way to the reception Jakari stated,
"I'm not waiting until tonight to lift this dress
up."

So as he's planting kisses from my
neck on down, I'm fondling with buttons to
try and figure out how to put the privacy
window up. He says, "Wife what are you
doing?"

I say, "Trying to put the privacy
window up?"

He says, "Damn that, I'm trying to
make a movie right now." Before I knew it,
we were cumming and the vehicle was
stopping. I knew everybody would be
wondering what we were doing, but we are
huge fans of power naps. So, we sat in the

limo for about twenty minutes before going in. Thank God for my travel bag that was already in the back seat, because we had some baby wipes to get us right for the moment. Don't judge us, we're nasty and we love each other.

While we were relaxing in the limo, Michelle called asking, "Should we start without y'all."

I said, "That's fine. I will give a five minutes heads up when we our on our way to the door." We assumed that by the time we were ready to go in, our wedding party should have been announced, and seated. Now, it would be time for the first dance. Once we gather ourselves, I sent Michelle a text to let her know that we are on our way into the venue. We stepped outside of the limo, both straightening our clothes, and

173

headed towards the entrance doors. Soon as we walk in, I hear Fiya yell out, "Y'all nasty!"

The spotlight was on us, and Jakari led us to the center of the dance floor and extended his right arm. I took his hand as we stood waving at our people, and the DJ announced, "I present to you Mr. and Mrs. Taylor for their first dance." The song that played was Charlie Wilson's, You Are, which meant a lot to me because it was the same song Jakari proposed to me with. We danced and cameras flashed, my eyes took a survey around the room, and I didn't see Shawn; I felt a little better.

We ate, drank, laughed, and danced the entire night. The joke of the day goes to the DJ; I heard that when my bridesmaids were coming out to Happy People by R.

Kelly, that he slapped his hand against his forehead and said, "I don't care what they say about this man, he still makes good music," and it had everybody laughing. The food was delicious, the drinks were great, and the vibe was priceless. I know it might seem cliché, but the night was unforgettable.

The next morning, we woke up in a king size bed in a luxury condo in Dubai. I rolled over to my right, and just watched as my husband slept, and I took a few seconds to admire the ring on my hand. But when I say a second, I meant that in a literal sense, because immediately I hopped up and went to the bathroom and was puking my guts up. I just felt like there was no way that I was over my limit, because I didn't even drink as much as I normally do. So, I washed my face, hopped in the shower, and then came out, and hopped on top of my husband. But twenty minutes in, I was running to the bathroom again.

This time Jakari followed me, and asked if I was okay, and I said I don't know because I just threw up a while ago before I came back to bed. He said, "How much did you drink last night?"

"Not that much."

"Are you sure?"

"Yeah, I only had a few drinks, and two of them were a glass of wine, and one was liquor."

Jakari jokingly says, "Well you know I've been trying to put a baby in you anyway, are you pregnant?"

And I stated, "Real fucking funny."

"Damn you cussing me out on our honeymoon?"

"No, but damn can't we be married for a while before starting a family?" And I couldn't even hear Jakari's response because I was throwing up again. So I stood in the shower letting the water run on my back for about fifteen minutes, until I thought I was fine. I got out, got dressed, and we went to the first convenient store we could find. I purchased a pregnancy test, some ibuprofen, a Sprite and some crackers. Swiftly I stuck the test in my purse without Jakari seeing it. The guy behind the counter seen me and added it to our total.

We then went directly back to the hotel, even though Jakari wanted to go site seeing. I told him that we had four more days for site seeing, and that I just didn't feel good today. When we walked in, I went straight to the bathroom, locked the door, and peed on the stick. Two to three minutes later, I found out I was going to be somebody's mom and I was surprisingly disappointed. Not because I didn't want to have a child with Jakari, just because I wasn't ready. So I stayed in the bathroom for a while contemplating about the future. I don't know how long I stayed in there, but I'm pretty sure I was in there for at least a half hour before I heard a knock on the door, and Jakari was asking if I was okay.

I angrily opened the door, and yelled, "Yeah I think I'm okay, but I think I'm pregnant."

"Why are you so upset?"

"Maybe because there's something that you haven't told me yet."

"Well if you think I'm keeping secrets, why did you get married then?"

"Because I love you, why else. So, is there anything you want to tell me?"

"Like what?"

"Like you fucked somebody else in our house?"

His eyes got all wide, and he yells out, "When… who?"

"Yup, I knew I should have said something before today because you don't know what I'm talking about, huh?"

"So you knew about this before today, before the wedding?"

And I looked at him like, duh. This guy begins to shed tears, and I said, "Answer me. So just like you were asking me all those

179

questions about Shawn, and demanding answers, answer the fucking question."

He says, "Chill out talking to me like that," and with tears rolling down his eyes, "Promise me no matter what I say, you'll stay. I can't believe you are upset about being pregnant and now you want to ruin our honeymoon over some old stuff. It was a mistake babe. Damn, I heard that females get emotional when they are pregnant, but you are tripping."

I yelled "TAAALLLKKKK"!

He said, "After that situation with Shawn, I started talking to this chick that I worked with about our relationship. Next thing you know I invited her over while you were at work. I ended up fucking her in the guest bathroom, and now she's pregnant too! Baby I couldn't imagine this, not in a million years, I am so sorry that this had to come out today when we are supposed to be celebrating our marriage. If I could take it all back, I would. I'm not sure what your thoughts are about this, but I even offered her money to get an abortion. I'm so sorry. Do you have anything at all to say to me? Say something please."

I said, "This shit feels like déjà vu. I remember feeling sick to my stomach the day I seen the condom in our guest bathroom. If you thought that I didn't see it, you are out of your mind. I tried to be the bigger person. I tried to push it to the side. I'm trying to love you and all of your flaws, but I can tell you right now that I'm not having your baby along with another chick. FUCK YOU! I SHOULD KILL YOU AND HER!" I busted out the bathroom and stormed past Jakari, straight to the kitchen and grabbed the first

C.T.

knife I saw. It was at this point that I realized that love could be DEADLY...

Made in the USA
Middletown, DE
17 June 2019